NINE, TEN ... NEVER SLEEP AGAIN NEVER SLEEP AGAIN

REBEKKA FRANCK, BOOK 5

WILLOW ROSE

Special thanks to my editor Jean Pacillo
http://www.ebookeditingpro.com

Cover design by Juan Villar Padron,
https://juanjjpadron.wixsite.com/juanpadron

Follow Willow Rose on BookBub:
https://www.bookbub.com/authors/willow-rose

Connect with Willow Rose:

willow-rose.net

PROLOGUE

AUGUST 2012

As usual, he couldn't sleep. It had become quite a big problem for him lately. Henrik Fenger had never been a heavy sleeper, but the last month or so he had hardly been able to sleep at all. He never fell asleep until early in the morning and then, only for a few hours. It was about to drive him crazy. He was tossing and turning in the hotel bed with the girl sleeping next to him. She had fallen asleep after the sex. Henrik thought it would make it easier for him to sleep if he had sex with her first. That was the whole point, but, as it turned out, she was the only one who had fallen asleep after three hours of him riding her in all kinds of positions. He had been rough with her; he knew that, which was why he decided to let her sleep a little, to recover first, before he sent her away.

Now he was having a new thought. Maybe it was her? Maybe he couldn't sleep because of her? Could it be guilt? Did her presence mess him up, because he felt bad for Janni at home alone with the kid as usual when Henrik was out on his business trips?

Henrik shook his head. Nah. That couldn't be why. He had done this a million times; hell he always brought back a hooker from the hotel lobby when he was out on business trips.

But, nevertheless, the girl had to go.

He poked her with his elbow hard in the side and she woke up with a gasp. "What's going on?" she moaned.

"You need to go," Henrik said.

"But it's three in the morning?"

"Grab your stuff. I've put money on the dresser for you." He said with a sigh.

"Money? What are you talking about?" The girl lifted her head and looked at him. "You think I'm some kind of hooker?"

"I don't know what you are and I don't care. Take the money or leave it, as long as you're out of here."

She looked at him, confused. "But how? How ... how can you think something like that after the night we had? After all the things you said? I thought ..." she got out of bed and stared at him. "I thought you were a nice guy. I thought we were having a nice time together."

"So what? You're expecting to get my phone number, is that it? You want to *get together* and hang out and eat *seaweed*, drink *smoothies* and discuss *gluten free diets*? Is that it?" he said with a shrill voice, pretending he was a girl.

The girl picked up her blouse from the floor. "You ripped this, by the way," she said. "It was pretty expensive."

Henrik looked away. "Buy yourself a new one with the money you earned tonight. You deserve it."

The girl grunted and put on her blouse, then her shoes. Henrik watched her as she bent down to get her other red, high-heeled shoe. She had long legs and a great ass. He would do her again right there on the floor; take her from behind, if it he didn't need to get some sleep soon. Important meeting tomorrow. Important investors who he couldn't blow off.

"You're a real asshole. Has anyone ever told you that?" she said, and put on her jacket.

Henrik smiled. "Oh yeah. Lots of people. Especially women."

The girl scoffed, opened the door, and left while mumbling something in anger.

"Bye bye now. Take care," he yelled after her with a grin.

Women. They all reacted the same way. How was he supposed to know she wasn't a hooker? She looked just like one. Wasn't that enough for him to assume she was one? And she certainly fucked like one, that was for sure. Oh boy, the things she had done for him. It was almost worth him seeing her a second time.

Well almost.

Henrik yawned and put his head back on the pillow. He really hoped he never ran into this girl again. Well, he was only in town this one night. Tomorrow he was off to Hamburg. A new town meant new women. There was always one who fell for his charm.

The last sucker isn't born yet.

Henrik closed his eyes and tried to sleep, but after half an hour he realized it wasn't going to happen on its own. Henrik grunted and looked at the clock. He only had three more hours before he had to get up. This was really annoying. He got out of bed and walked to his suitcase on the floor. He searched through it, but didn't find what he was looking for. Henrik remembered he had put his toilet bag in the bathroom. He walked in there and spotted the bottle of sleeping pills that he was looking for. But they weren't in the bag next to the sink, as he assumed they would be. No, they were in the hand of a person wearing a doctor's mask, juggling the bottle, making the pills rattle inside of it.

"Looking for these?" the person said. "Can't sleep can we?"

"Who ... Who are you and what are you doing in here? You can't be in here!" Henrik said angrily. Who the hell was this person? A dream? Had he finally fallen asleep? He hadn't heard anyone enter his room.

"Who are you?" he repeated when he spotted a syringe in the person's other hand. Faster than he could react, the needle was pierced through the skin on Henrik's shoulder and the liquid inside of it was injected into his arm, while the person behind the mask said:

"I'm your next nightmare."

1

AUGUST 2012

"ARE WE THERE YET?"

The question came from Julie in the backseat of Peter's car. I turned to look at her. "Just half an hour more," I said.

"I can't wait," she replied with a wide smile. It warmed my heart to see the joy in her eyes. She had been so happy lately, ever since her dad and I decided to give our relationship another try.

"Me either," I said and turned to look out the window again at the beautiful hills and forests. The corn in the fields had just been harvested and autumn was right around the corner. We had taken Julie out of school for a week to all go away to Peter's family estate outside of Aarhus. Peter and I had a lot of healing to do in our relationship and we figured the entire family would benefit from a trip away together, just spending time with each other.

We needed it and Julie, in particular, needed it. Her relationship with her father suffered from the fact that she was a little afraid of him, still. Peter had lost it back when he got back from Iraq and, along with taking too many pills, he had gone crazy and once locked us both inside the basement of our old house. After years in treatment, he was now doing better; the medicine was gone, and along with it, the anger. We had been doing very well for a month and a half now and it was time to mend the broken pieces, we both agreed.

I had never been to the estate by Lake Brabrand before and was looking forward to finally seeing it. It had been in Peter's family for several generations, but he and his brother fought too much to be able to share it properly and Peter had backed out many years ago. But now, the brother had moved to Spain and left it to Peter to take care of. Peter had been coming there a lot to get away from everything and he had told me the place made him feel better, the quietness, the nature, it had helped him clear his mind and make the changes he needed to get better. It had been like therapy to him. And, as far as I could see, it had done wonders. Peter was just like the Peter I had fallen in love with when I first met him during my stay in Iraq, working as a reporter many years ago. He was sweet and caring towards the both of us and I sensed a sadness in him, as well, for having treated us badly when he wasn't well. He felt like he had to make up for it somehow and that made him sweeter than ever.

"I can't wait to play in the yard," Julie said. "You should see it, Mom. It's huge. Like really huge, like an entire forest surrounding the castle."

Julie insisted on calling the place a castle. It was so sweet; she was so easy to impress. "I bet it's great for hide and seek," I said.

"It is, Mom. It's perfect. You'll never find me."

I laughed and looked at my daughter. Her blue eyes were sparkling. I felt a tender pinch in my heart from love. I really enjoyed being a family again. It felt somehow so right.

Peter smiled. "We're almost there now."

He took the exit and got off the highway. We drove for a long time through forests. I thought about my dad. We had left him back at the house, but he hadn't been well. I felt bad for leaving him like this, but he had told me he was fine. I had called my sister to check in on him now and then. She lived fifteen minutes away so it wasn't too big a request, even if she thought it was.

"I have a life too," she said when I called to ask if she could do this for me. "I have kids who needs to be picked up and dropped off, I have gymnastics, swimming and soccer practice, plus I work full time," she had argued.

"It's just for one week," I said. "We really need to have some time alone as a family if we want this to work. As it is now, Peter is living in a hotel and stopping by every day to be with us. We need some time to see if we're able to move in together. We need to work on our relationship to become a family again. Just do it for me, okay?"

My sister sighed profoundly. "Alright. I'll do it for you. And for dad. Not for Peter. You know I hate that guy for what he did to you."

"I know. But please promise me that you'll work on forgiving him. If I can, then I think you can too."

My sister exhaled. "Well, maybe I will. Eventually."

"We're here!" Julie shrieked from the backseat and pulled me out of my reverie. I lifted my eyes and looked out the front window. Then I dropped my jaw, literally. It was stunning. Placed in the middle of the lake on a small island was a huge white mansion surrounded by trees.

"Wow," I exclaimed. "It really is a castle."

"I told you, Mom. I told you it was."

"How do we get out there?" I asked. It seemed to be placed in the middle of the water.

"I have a small boat," Peter said.

As he parked the car by the shore, I spotted the small boat in the water. I had to say I was pretty intrigued. I was looking forward to being in a secluded area with my family with no distractions to keep us away from each other. And I certainly got what I wished for.

2

JANUARY 1995

WHEN VALDEMAR WAS BORN, his mother knew right away that something was wrong. The nurses and doctors wouldn't give him to her and kept turning their backs on her, talking amongst themselves, shaking their heads.

"What's wrong?" Anna asked with a shivering voice. "Why can't I see him? Why won't you give him to me?"

Finally, a doctor turned and gazed at her. His face looked grave and she embraced herself for what he was going to say. Anna could hear the boy cry, so he was alive, that wasn't it, he wasn't born dead. What else could it be that was so terrible that they wouldn't tell her? That they would keep the child away from her? The same child she had been waiting for for so long, wanting so desperately to finally hold in her arms, and then couldn't. Why? Anna simply didn't understand. As the doctor looked at her with his serious eyes, she felt her heart rate go up.

Just say it, for crying out loud.

"There is something that you need to know," the doctor started.

"What's wrong? Is he sick?" Anna asked.

The doctor avoided her eyes. His mouth turned down. "You could say that, but it's not ... well it's a little different."

"What is it? Just say it." Anna said, her voice creaking in desperation.

"Well it seems that your boy has ... an abnormality."

"What kind of abnormality?"

"Well, it seems that he ... he is missing both of his arms."

Anna fell backwards in the hospital bed. She felt confused. Dumbfounded even. "He's what? What do you mean he is missing his arms?"

"I mean that he was born without arms. We really don't understand why the sonograms failed to reveal these complications."

Anna stared at the doctor with disbelief. She tried really hard, but still couldn't understand what he was saying. How could the baby have no arms?

"I ... I ... I don't ..."

How will he eat? How will he get by? Will the arms grow out eventually? She had so many questions at that particular moment, but couldn't get the words across her lips. *How are we going to do this? What will Michael say?*

"The father is in the waiting room still, I assume?" the doctor asked.

Anna nodded. A nurse turned to look at her. "Are you ready to see him?" she asked. In her eyes, Anna saw nothing but pity for Anna's situation. Anna didn't care much for that. It made her feel pitiful. And you're not supposed to feel pitiful when you've just given birth to a child, are you? It was supposed to be a time of joy for her and her husband, a time of blessed happiness, wasn't it?

Anna looked at the nurse skeptically. Did she really want to see him? Did she really want this crippled child who could never do anything on his own?

She thought about saying no. For just a short second, she wondered if she could get out of here, get out of this nightmare somehow, maybe if she just jumped out of the bed and started running now? What would happen if she simply left?

"Here he is," the nurse said and handed her a small bundle before Anna could make her decision.

The bundle was so light, so small she was afraid to break what was in it. Anna felt tears press from behind her eyes and tried hard to force them back, just as the baby opened his eyes and looked at her. In that instant Anna knew her life *was* really changed forever and would never be the same again. Tears rolled across her cheeks as she stroked the boy on the head. Never in her life had she ever seen anything like this boy; never in her life had she felt anything like what she felt at that instant. Looking into those very blue eyes of his changed everything.

Arms or no arms, Anna was in love.

3

AUGUST 2012

WHEN HENRIK FENGER OPENED his eyes he didn't remember where he was. He blinked a couple of times to focus better. The light in the bathroom felt very bright.

The bathroom? What am I doing in the bathroom? Last night? What happened last night? There was someone in here. There was someone in the bathroom?

Henrik felt suddenly anxious and turned his head to look around him. He realized he was sitting in the bathtub. What was he doing in the bathtub? Had he been sleeping in there? Why? Henrik felt suddenly so thirsty, like he hadn't had anything to drink for days. His tongue was dry and felt sticky inside his mouth. He was groggy, his thoughts clouded, and he could hardly focus. Suddenly, he realized he was very cold and looked down only to discover that his body was covered in ice, all the way up to his chest.

Where the hell did all this ice come from? A bucket next to the bathtub gave him a clue. The ice had to come from the machine in the hallway outside. But why? Why would anyone sink him into ice? Henrik now remembered the needle the person had held in their hand and injected into his arm. It was still sore and there was a small mark from where it had gone through the skin. What had been in that needle? Henrik felt so groggy and had to fight to stay awake. He felt confused. It was so hard to figure out what was going on. Just moving his arm to pull it above the ice took a lot of work. It was just like the time when he had his appendix removed and he had to be put under anesthesia. The waking up was so hard. All he wanted was to go back to sleep. Getting back to reality felt like being punched in the face.

Henrik groaned and tried to move his body underneath the ice, but it was difficult. *You need to get up from this cold ice or you'll freeze to death. Move your body. Come on, Henrik. Just do it.*

Henrik blinked his eyes and looked up when he spotted something on the white wall in front of him. He blinked again to be able to focus better and soon he realized it was a note. It was taped to the wall. It wasn't hard for him to read it. In big letters it simply said:

DON'T MOVE. CALL 112.

Henrik blinked again trying hard to figure out what this was all about. Was it a dream? Some weird psychedelic nightmare? It had to be. It simply had to be. Had the person drugged him and that was why he was dreaming this strange dream?

Henrik shook his head. It was hurting badly now.

No, this is no dream. This is real. This is very real.

Henrik turned his head and spotted a small table that had been placed next to the bathtub with his cellphone on top of it. Something felt weird, he thought to himself. Something was different when he tried to move, to turn his torso. The ice numbed it, but it still hurt. Henrik was struck by a strange feeling and reached back his hand to try and touch his back. He pressed his hand slowly and carefully through the ice.

Something is really wrong here.

Henrik didn't dare to touch it anymore. He pulled his hand back with a gasp. Carefully he reached for the phone and dialed the emergency number, 112.

"What's your emergency?" the lady asked.

Henrik felt his heart beat faster and had to focus in order to not lose consciousness. "I ... I think something bad happened to me. Please send an ambulance."

"What happened to you sir?"

Henrik moaned. The pain in his back was getting worse by the second now. The anesthesia was wearing off and the ice didn't do much to help him anymore. The realization of what had happened to him was slowly sinking in and it hurt more than anything.

"Sir? Are you still there? What's your emergency? Sir? Can you speak? Are you still there?"

"Yes," he said with drops of sweat springing from his forehead, sweat from excruciating pain. "Yes. I'm here."

"I'm sending an ambulance right away. What's happened?" the woman asked again.

Henrik moaned heavily while seeing black spots in front of his eyes.

"I ... I think ... someone removed something from inside of me."

4

"Do you like it?"

Peter looked at me as he opened the gate to the driveway. In front of us rose the enormous white house. It was beautiful.

"Love it," I answered. We walked towards the house with our bags. "Why is there a driveway if you can only get here by boat?" I asked.

"The lake is not very deep on this side towards the land. Sometimes in the summer when the water level is low, you can drive here. You need an SUV, since it gets really muddy. I've done it a couple of times."

"Yeah, we did it together, me and daddy when we were here last time," Julie said and ran ahead of us towards the main entrance of the house.

"Oh you did, now did you?" I said, a little dissatisfied that I hadn't heard about this before.

Peter led us to the courtyard. A broad set of stairs led to the front entrance, a massive old wooden door. It was stunning. Everything about this place was stunning. Magnificent, even. I had never been in a place like this before.

Peter found the keys and opened the door for us. "Ladies first," he said with a smirk.

Julie stormed inside and I followed her. If it was splendid from the outside it was nothing compared to what it was on the inside. It was simply breathtaking. The high ceilings that seemed endless, the marble floors, the paintings on the walls as big as Julie, the stairwell leading upstairs, the many hallways leading to unknown places. It was incredible.

I looked at Peter. "You'd better show the way," I said. "I don't want to get lost in this massive house."

Peter chuckled, then walked towards the stairs. We followed him. "Julie and I stayed in two rooms up here the last time. They were great, weren't they sweetheart?"

Julie nodded eagerly.

"How many rooms are there?" I asked.

"Fifty-two without the servants' quarters in the back."

"You're kidding me, right?"

Peter laughed. "Of course I am. It's only forty-eight if you don't count the servants' quarters in the back."

"Very funny."

Peter laughed. "It's true. I'm not lying."

"That's a lot of rooms. How old is it?" I asked.

"It's very old. It was built by a bishop many years ago, in 1302. During the reformation, in 1536, it was taken over by the king who used it as a prison. It has been told that a famous Scottish Earl was put in this prison and went insane. He killed himself in here. They say that at night you can still hear the horse driven carriage that carried his body away, but I've never heard it. Later it became a mental institution for a short period from 1840 to 1857. My great-grandfather bought it in 1901 when it had been empty for a couple of years. He completely restored it back to its old splendor when it used to be a Renaissance castle in the beginning." Peter walked down the hallway and stopped in front of a door. "This is Julie's room," he said. "This is where she slept the last time we were here."

"Yay," Julie said and opened the door to her room. I peeked in. It looked like a nice big bed in there. The furniture was very old and dark. Julie threw her bag and then herself on the bouncy bed. I smiled. She seemed to feel so at home here.

"Now you and I will be in the room right next to hers," Peter said.

I followed him down the hallway. "You and I, huh? You really think we're ready for that?"

Peter opened the door and showed me the most astonishing room. It was huge, almost the size of my dad's entire first floor. It had a big bathroom attached to it with a spa and, in the center, was literally the biggest bed I had ever seen. It was all very old-fashioned but astoundingly beautiful.

"Don't you think we are now?" he asked. "Don't you think we're ready to take this to the next level?"

I took off my shoes and planted my feet in the thick carpet. Then I smiled. "I think we are." I walked closer, then leaned over and kissed him. "I really think we are."

5

JANUARY 1995

VALDEMAR LOOKED UP AT Anna with his big blue eyes. Anna couldn't help crying, not because of the fact that he had no arms, no. She had already completely forgotten all about that and all she wanted was to take her baby home. No, she was crying because, at that moment, holding him in her arms at the hospital, she was happier than she had ever been in her life. Finally she felt complete, finally she felt like her life had a meaning, a purpose.

She couldn't stop smiling and stroking him gently across his face, putting her finger on his small nose.

The doctor kept talking about what their options were, how they would get help from the county to make their home handicap-friendly and help to take care of the baby in any way needed and that they could provide a therapist to help the family cope with this tragedy and burden that had come upon them.

Anna had stopped listening a long time ago. How could anyone ever think that little boy could be a burden to her? How could he be anything but a blessing to them?

"I'll go get the father now," the doctor said and left.

Anna hardly noticed he was gone. She kept looking at her baby boy, Valdemar, who stared back at her with his wondrous eyes. Much to her surprise, he had stopped crying as soon as he was handed to her. And ever since she had held him in her arms, he had been smiling, which was really special and surprising, since Anna had read in her books preparing to become a mother, than newborns didn't smile until weeks after they were born.

That was when Anna first realized that Valdemar was a very special child.

"Anna!" Michael stormed into the room. He was pale and looked confused. "How are you?"

She lifted her head and looked at him. His eyes were overwhelmed with fear and worry. "The doctor told me," he said.

Anna smiled. She lifted the baby higher so he could better see him. Michael smiled insecurely. "Can I see?" he said.

Anna nodded. Michael grabbed the blanket and unwrapped the boy's shoulders. He gasped. Then his facial expression changed drastically and he stepped backwards while shaking his head. "No," he said.

"Michael," Anna said. "It will be okay. We'll figure it out together. Like we always do, remember?"

But Michael didn't remember. He kept shaking his head, staring at the boy's missing arms with a strange expression to his face, which Anna didn't care for. She hurriedly re-covered the boy's shoulders with the blanket and pulled him close to her body again. Michael stared at her like he was appalled by her and the very fact that she was able to care for such a misshapen creature, like it made him feel disgusted by her.

"Michael?" she said with a shiver to her voice. "It's going

to be okay. He's still our boy. He's still the Valdemar we have been waiting for."

Michael shook his head. "No. No. That is not my son."

"Michael?" Anna was crying now. "How can you say such a thing? He's still your son and will always be."

"No," Michael simply said, then turned around and walked away.

Anna cried. Her entire body was shivering in anger and desperation. "Michael!" she cried out after him, and finally he turned to face her again. In his eyes she saw something she would never forget for the rest of her life.

She saw blame. He was blaming her for what had happened. He was blaming her for giving birth to a boy without arms. She gasped and leaned back against the pillow. Never had she seen such resentment in her beloved's eyes. Never had she seen such anger and disappointment. It hurt in every bone of her body.

"Michael?" she said.

But he never answered.

6

AUGUST 2012

"IT SEEMS THAT YOU'VE had your kidney removed."

The doctor standing next to Henrik Fenger's bed looked like a pig, Henrik thought. He was big and fat and had almost pink skin. And then there was the nose. It somehow reminded Henrik of a pig with the big nostrils. He was repulsed by this person and even more by what he was now telling him.

"My kidney?" he asked. "How the hell ...? Henrik felt dizzy and had to close his eyes for a second.

"It was very professionally done, so whoever did it must have tried something like this before."

"Wha ...? What? How? I want to know how this could have happened. I demand to know!" Henrik had to hold back his rage. Now that he had become clearer in his head, he felt nothing but anger for what had happened and he wanted those behind it to pay.

"Well you were probably heavily sedated first. That's why you didn't feel anything. But I really feel you should discuss all this with the police when they get here."

"But what about my kidney?"

"You'll be fine with only one. Lots of people live perfect lives with just one kidney."

"But where the hell is it now? Why would anyone want to take my kidney?" Henrik was snorting in furor now.

The doctor shrugged. "I really feel you should talk to the police about the details. I don't know much about it."

"Then get the fucking police here right now!" Henrik yelled.

The doctor left and came back with a nurse who gave Henrik something *to calm him down*, the doctor said.

Henrik protested. "I don't want to be calm. I'm angry. I want to see these people hung and tortured for what they've done ..."

"You really shouldn't get this agitated Mr. Fenger," the nurse said. "Your body can't cope with it."

"Don't tell me what to do and what not to do. I am angry and I am entitled to be very, very angry!" Henrik rose from the bed and stormed towards the nurse with his hands towards her, grabbing her around the throat, screaming and yelling. Suddenly he felt dizzy once again and, shortly after, everything went black. The last thing he heard was the nurse scream.

When Henrik opened his eyes again, he was strapped to the bed and could hardly move his hands. "I'm sorry, Mr. Fenger but we had to strap you down," the piggy doctor told him. "You attacked one of our nurses and we can't have that happening again."

Henrik tried to pull his arms and legs loose, but couldn't. He groaned and yelled in anger. "How dare you? I'm the victim here!"

"The police are here and ready to talk to you, when you're calm enough."

Henrik moaned and fought with the straps.

"I guess I can always tell them to come back later," the doctor continued.

"No. No. Please don't. I'll stay calm," Henrik pleaded, then drew in a deep breath. "I'm calm now. I'm calm."

"Good. That's better. Your body can't sustain those bursts of anger, Mr. Fenger. You have to try and stay calm."

Henrik nodded. "I will. I promise."

"Good. I'll let them know then," the doctor said and left him.

As the minutes passed, Henrik fought to stay calm, but it was really hard. This whole situation left him with such an excruciating anger, one that he usually only showed towards his wife and kid at home behind closed doors. He never lost it at work or in front of strangers. But this ... this ... was just too much for him to be able to restrain himself.

"Mr. Fenger?"

Two officers entered his room. They looked like idiots. Just like all other police officers Henrik had ever encountered. Was the entire police force all morons? Henrik took a couple of deep breaths to stay calm. "Yes," he said, trying really hard to smile.

The officer looked down at his notepad. He looked like it annoyed him to be there. As if Henrik's case was beneath him. It made Henrik even more furious.

"We have been updated on your most unfortunate situation by Doctor Hansen ..."

"There is nothing *unfortunate* about my situation," Henrik said through gritted teeth.

"Excuse me?"

"What?"

"You said something?"

"Well, you used the word unfortunate and I didn't like that."

"You didn't like my choice of words?"

"No. My situation isn't unfortunate," Henrik said, trying really hard to restrain himself from exploding.

"Then, what is it?" the officer asked.

"It's a CRIME," Henrik yelled. "It's a fucking crime that someone has to pay big-time for."

The officer nodded. "That's what I meant. We agree, then. This unfortunate crime has to be investigated, of course, and Officer Frandsen and myself, Officer Jansson, will be the ones to do just that."

Henrik stared at the two buffoons in front of him. *Christ, here I am in fucking pain, the worst trouble in my life and these are the guys I have to depend on? Freaking Starsky and Hutch?*

"So what is your take on this?" He asked.

The two buffoons looked at each other. "Our take? I'm not sure I understand," officer Jansson said.

"What do you make of this? Of what happened to me? Who did this and why?" Henrik said, trying hard not to yell again.

Officer Jansson nodded. "Oh yes. Well we're probably talking about organ theft here."

You think?

"Okay. I kind of figured that out myself," Henrik said with a sigh. "Since someone stole one of my organs, that is. But what I meant is, do you have any idea who might have done this to me and, more importantly, do you have any idea how to find them and make them pay?"

Officer Frandsen cleared his throat. Henrik looked at him expectantly, hoping for just a small glimpse of hope.

"To be frank, we don't," he said. "As far as we know this is a first in this country. Organ theft is mostly seen in Eastern European and Asian countries."

"So you have no idea who took my kidney?" Henrik said, flabbergasted.

Both officers shook their heads. "I'm afraid we don't, no," one of them said. Henrik didn't care who.

"Were you alone in the room?" Officer Janssen asked.

Henrik hesitated. He could hardly tell them about the girl, now could he? *The girl?* Could it? Could it be her? It had to be. It had to be her. She had to have something to do with this. But he couldn't tell Starsky and Hutch here, could he? 'Cause then his wife would find out. Then she would leave him and take Thomas with her like she had sworn she would if he ever cheated on her again. No, he couldn't risk that.

"So ... what do we do next?" he asked.

The officers looked at each other again, then at Henrik. "Well first, *we* take your statement and then *we* have to get back to the station and see what *we* can do," Officer Frandsen said. "We will start an investigation and get in contact with our Eastern European contacts to help us. We suggest that you stay here at the hospital till they're ready to let you out and then you go on to live your life like you used to. We'll be in touch."

After they left, Henrik stared for a long time at the door. It was in those crucial minutes following that he slowly realized that it was time to take matters into his own hands.

7

AUGUST 2012

THOMAS DE QUINCEY WAS looking through pictures on his computer. Pictures of a woman lying on the ground somewhere, her dead eyes staring at the photographer, her mouth stuck in a scream, her hand cut off and stuffed into her mouth making it look like she was throwing up her own hand. He studied it closely. The pool of blood gave the picture great color, but the girl didn't do anything for him. He wasn't appalled, he wasn't disgusted or delighted.

Thomas De Quincey leaned back in his chair and tilted his head slightly to look at it differently, but it still didn't do anything. The creator, the artist of this piece claimed it was worth a lot of money. Two hundred and fifty thousand, he wrote in his e-mail. With the deal, Thomas would get the girl and the hand in the mouth and that was quite unique. Thomas had never seen anything like this before. But he couldn't help wondering if the girl had already been dead when the artist put the hand in? 'Cause that would change everything. If she was still alive, then it had the cruelty and gruesomeness that he was looking for, but if she was simply killed, and then the artist had cut off the hand and stuck it in her mouth for effect, then it was worth nothing to Thomas. And he simply didn't get the vibe from it he was looking for. It didn't cause the hairs to stand up on his back. It didn't have the brutality to it to make him shiver in delight. It simply wasn't there.

Thomas closed the picture and checked the chat. He had recently received a new follower, a new member who he had tutored and he was very excited to hear news from him and what he was about to do. He called himself Bill Durgin after the famous photographer whose macabre pictures were well-known to those, like Thomas De Quincey, who enjoyed the macabre immensely and lived for it.

Thomas chuckled when he saw that his new apprentice was online. He had that same feeling of excitement he used to have back when he had let Fred Einaudi, alias Allan Witt become a part of his small, yet very exclusive, club. Thomas broke a pencil thinking about how things had ended with Allan. Thomas had been very careful taking in a new member this time, in order to not make the same mistake twice. Allan had simply been too crazy and finally lost it completely. It was too dangerous to have someone that unstable as a part of the group. But, with the kind of people he attracted, it was probably hard to avoid.

This one, he was pretty sure, wouldn't let him down. He had passed all of Thomas' test and questionnaires. His fantasies were quite different from those Thomas usually encountered, since he wasn't as interested in actually killing, as he was in just simply inflicting immense pain on a special group of people. This was a new approach and very very intriguing. Thomas was extremely excited to see where this Bill Durgin was going to take it.

How did it go? Thomas wrote.

Perfect, Bill Durgin answered. *It went exactly as I had hoped.*

Bill Durgin went quiet, then posted some pictures. Thomas looked at them, feeling thrilled. He clapped his hands like he was applauding him, then wrote: *Good. I'm so happy to hear that. Don't forget to give me my payment.*

I won't. Next time. I promise.

When will you strike next?

Tomorrow night.

How exciting. Good luck.

Thanks.

Then he was gone. Thomas saw that two of his other apprentices were on as well. He wondered if he should write to them, but decided to just watch as they talked to one another instead. It was his chat forum, he had created it and he could listen in on his member's conversations any time without them knowing it. They were discussing a kill that one of them had done two nights ago. One of them was posting pictures while the other was jerking off watching them. The display on Thomas' phone lit up. He had received a text. Thomas looked at it:

Your delivery is here, it simply said.

8

AUGUST 2012

I SLEPT WONDERFULLY THAT night in the big bed. Peter woke me up with kisses and touches.

"Not now," I groaned, hoping desperately to get to sleep just for a little longer. I felt his hand on my thigh and his kisses on my throat. It felt good.

"Just a quick one," he whispered and put his hand inside my panties.

"Mmm," I moaned and let him crawl on top of me.

"Mmm you smell good," he moaned. "You taste even better."

I chuckled, but stopped as he came inside of me. I held his head between my hands and stared into his blue eyes. I felt so happy to be back with him. I hadn't realized how much I had missed him, how deeply I still loved him. Making love to him again reminded me of how much I liked us, how much we belonged together even if it meant having to fight through bad times.

I took a shower before breakfast and Peter went down to the kitchen to start cooking for us. Julie was already awake, he told me before he left the bedroom. She was running around in the yard, playing hide and seek with her imaginary friend.

"She has an imaginary friend?" I asked. Why hadn't I heard about that?

"I think he arrived the last time she was up here. I guess he lives here or something. Maybe he's just an animal, who knows?"

"I hope she won't get lost out there," I said.

"It's an island, Rebekka," Peter said with a grin. "We'll find her if she is lost. Don't you worry."

I heard her squeal in laughter from the yard and peeked out through the bathroom window. Then I laughed. Julie was running in circles, laughing out loud. I wiped myself with the towel thinking this stay was going to do all of us good.

I grabbed my toilet bag and started unpacking my stuff in the bathroom, putting things on the shelves in the cabinet above the sink. I pulled out a pack of tampons and looked at them. I was terrible at keeping track of when I was supposed to have my period. When I had been trying to get pregnant with Sune I had tried to be systematic about it. I had written in my calendar when I had my period but always ended up forgetting a month and then it was all messed up. Sune had been really annoyed with that.

I put the box on the shelf in the bathroom, then walked back into the room. I got dressed while looking at myself in the mirror. Had I gained weight?

No you're just acting crazy again. You always think you've gained weight. Learn to live with it. Make peace with your thighs.

I put on my jeans and a shirt and went downstairs. It took awhile for me to find the kitchen and Peter. He smiled when I entered.

"Right on time," he said.

"In time for what?" I asked, when the smell of food hit my nostrils and I realized I was starving.

"Breakfast is on the table."

He wasn't kidding. On the table was everything I loved. Scrambled eggs, croissants, buns and soft boiled eggs.

"You didn't make all this?" I asked. In all the many years of us being married he had never cooked for me before. Not even boiled an egg.

Peter smiled. "Nah," he said. "I have help. Mrs. Holm. She was here early this morning and made it all. She cooked for the entire day, so we only have to warm it up. She'll be back tomorrow morning."

"Of course you have help," I said with a grin and sank my teeth into a croissant. It was heavenly. "Does she come every day?"

"Not on weekends. Her husband loves to fish, so he keeps his boat on the dock on the shore that she uses to get here every day."

"Does she clean the entire place as well?" I asked, feeling suddenly sorry for this poor lady, with all the many rooms and bathrooms.

Peter chuckled. "No. She puts on new bed sheets and stuff in the rooms we use, but she doesn't clean. I have a cleaning company that I hire to do that."

"Of course you do." I grabbed another croissant happily, forgetting all about how fat I thought I looked in the mirror less than half an hour ago. I chewed while looking at Peter. He was so handsome. He drank his coffee, holding the cup between his big hands. I loved his big hands. I loved that he was so much man and nothing like ... I sighed and looked out the window where I spotted Julie in the yard. I hadn't spoken to Sune in weeks now and I felt really bad about how it had ended. I thought that if I gave him some time to heal, then maybe he would one day be able to forgive me. I didn't expect us to be friends again since he was so angry with me, but part of me still hoped we could ... someday. Julie had been asking a lot for Tobias and it was getting harder and harder for me to find reasons why we couldn't see each other, why I couldn't just call Sune and ask him to come over with Tobias like I used to.

The back door to the kitchen opened and Julie stormed in. Her cheeks were red from the cold wind and fresh air, her eyes sparkling with joy.

"Are you coming out to play?" she asked us.

I looked at Peter and shrugged. "Why not?" I asked. "It's not like I have something else to do today. How about you?"

Peter stretched himself with a long yawn. "I was actually planning on getting some painting done."

"Painting?" I asked. "Don't you have people to do that for you?"

Peter grinned. Julie made a disappointed sound.

"No not painting the walls, but real painting on canvas. I have created a studio for myself in the attic."

I almost dropped my fork. Peter painting? The idea was so strange to me. Peter the military man who had spend his entire life in war? First as a soldier, then by running his own private military security company that was, in fact, a mercenary company, making money off of war.

"Why did you start painting all of a sudden?" I asked.

"It all began some months ago," he said. "It is all a part of my therapy. I paint my emotions, so to speak. It's really soothing for me. Makes me calm and relaxed, I discovered. You know I've never been good at expressing myself and how I feel. This helps me deal with some of the stuff I carry around with me."

I stared at him thinking I hardly recognized the Peter I had once been married to. Was it really possible for someone to change this much?

"Surprised?" he asked.

"To put it mildly, yes."

Peter laughed again. "What can I say? It makes me happy. Painting makes me a better person."

"Good for you. I really mean that. I'd love to see them. I'd love to see your paintings."

Peter exhaled. "And you will. When I'm ready to show you. Right now I'm keeping them to myself, but someday ..."

"No pressure, Peter. It's okay. Just when you're ready for it. I know that kind of thing is sensitive. It's hard to put yourself and your work out there for people to see and criticize. Don't worry. I won't pressure you into showing me."

"Will you come out and play then, Mom?" Julie asked. "Please?"

I looked at her. "I'll come out and play in a few moments. I just want to catch up on the news first. I might be on vacation, but I still need to keep up with what's going on."

9

JANUARY 1997

It was Valdemar's second birthday. Anna was preparing the cake in the kitchen, putting whipped cream on top and setting the candles in the middle of it, while Valdemar was sitting on the floor looking up at her with affection in his eyes.

She smiled and looked down at him. "It's almost done, Valdemar. It's gonna be perfect, absolutely perfect."

Valdemar grinned, then bent forward and picked up a toy car between his teeth and started playing with it, using his mouth to push it around. Anna felt such great love for him at that instant. He had been finding his own ways to do things ever since he had started moving around on his feet. Crawling had been too much of a challenge without the arms to support him, so he had skipped that step and started walking at the age of seven months. One morning, while Anna and he had been sitting on the floor, he had suddenly bitten onto the bars of the playpen and pulled himself up with help from his mouth. Anna had gasped, thinking at first that something was wrong with him, since that was what Michael kept telling her.

"The boy is wrong. He is a mistake. He should never have been born. He will never be able to do anything. He'll need help just to eat for the rest of his life. What kind of a life is that for a child? And who will help him when he's a grown up? No one. He'll have to live in a home."

But at that instant, on the floor with seven month old Valdemar pulling himself up to an upright position using his mouth instead of hands, Anna realized that maybe, just maybe Michael was wrong about the boy. Suddenly, he was standing up next to the playpen with a huge smile and that was when he took his first step towards Anna with a big grin. At that moment, Anna cried and held out her arms and let him walk right into her embrace where she held him tightly for a long time, tickling his tummy, telling him how absolutely wonderful he was, how beautiful he was and how he would be able to do anything in life ... anything and no one should ever tell him differently.

And she had kept telling him that every day of his life ever since. She knew, in her heart, that this boy wasn't normal, and she thanked God every day for it. No, he wasn't normal, he was special. And he was going to do special things in this world. Things no one else would ever do or dare.

"Mommy?" he said and stood up.

"Yes sweetie?"

"Will daddy come home for my birthday?" Anna looked at her boy, then kneeled in front of him. She stroked his light hair between her fingers and looked into his eyes. What she saw in there didn't belong to a two-year old. No, Valdemar had clever eyes, eyes that had seen much, eyes that understood more than what a two-year old normally would. The way he talked told Anna that he was smarter than other kids, even if many people thought he was retarded because of the way he looked and moved. His language was much more developed than any other two-year old's. The doctor had told her and she heard it every day, how fast it developed and how long the sentences were that he was able to say. He was always using bigger and bigger words, sometimes so big Anna had to look them up to know what he meant.

"No, sweetie," she said looking into those eyes that seemed like they belonged to someone who was carrying the troubles of the world.

Just like last year, Michael wasn't going to be there to celebrate Valdemar's birthday. It was too difficult for him since he viewed this day as the darkest day in his life, not as the happiest like Anna. Like last year, he would probably go directly to the local bar in Brabrand after work and drink till he passed out and someone put him in a cab home. But even if Valdemar would understand all that if she explained it to him, she didn't want to. She saw every day how the gap between the boy and his father grew wider, how Valdemar looked at his father with longing eyes in the morning at the breakfast table, desperate for him to just look at him or even speak a few words to him.

But he never did. Michael ignored the fact that Valdemar even existed. And he had done so ever since they had come home from the hospital. He never picked him up. He never changed a diaper or even spoke to the boy. He simply pretended like he didn't exist and Valdemar didn't have to be as bright as he was to feel it, to sense his dad's resentment towards him. It was so obvious it hurt in every bone of Anna's body and some days she wished Michael would wait to come home from work till Valdemar was in his bed sleeping, to spare the boy from the pain of looking at his father without him looking back, of talking to him, asking him things and the father never answering. It was heartbreaking and she was tired of making excuses for him, yet she still did. Luckily for her and Valdemar, Michael's job as a salesman for a big toy company demanded that he travelled a lot and was often gone for weeks at a time.

"Daddy had a trip," she said, like she had said so many times before. And, like so many times before, she saw the small light of hope in her son's eyes slowly die out.

10

AUGUST 2012

JULIE RAN BACK outside and Peter went upstairs to paint while I pulled out my iPad. The national TV Station TV2's web-page was filled with yellow blocks stating *Breaking News*. I opened the link to watch it online. The anchor looked serious as she spoke.

"And now we will go live to the hospital in Aarhus where my colleague is with Henrik Fenger," she said.

Then they clipped to a live interview with some guy in a hospital bed. "Yes," the journalist on the spot said, "... and Henrik Fenger, I can understand you're very angry about what happened to you?"

"Of course I am," the man in the bed snorted. "Who wouldn't be?"

"Could you explain to us exactly what happened?" The journalist asked. On the screen the text said *Organ thieves stole man's kidney*.

"Well I ... I was trying to fall asleep and, when I couldn't, I walked into the bathroom at the hotel where I was staying ..."

"The Hotel Kragen in Brabrand," the journalist interrupted him.

"Hotel Kragen in Brabrand?" I mumbled. "I think we passed that place on our way here."

The man looked angry for being interrupted and shot the journalist a look that could kill. "Yes, the Hotel Kragen where I was staying for the night because I had an important meeting in the town the next morning."

"When did you realize your kidney was gone?" The journalist once again interrupted him.

"Well if you'd let me tell my story ..." the man stopped himself. It was obvious he fought to calm himself down. "I noticed someone was in my room as I went into the bathroom and I think I saw someone holding a syringe in their hand, an injection needle. That's all I remember ..."

"Were you alone?"

"What?"

"Were you sleeping alone in the hotel room?"

The man in the bed went quiet. He stared at the journalist with frozen eyes. "Of course," he said finally, after a long, slightly embarrassing, pause. "Of course I was alone. My wife and family were at home in Roskilde. I was away on a business trip."

"So when did you realize your kidney was missing?" The journalist asked.

"'The next morning I woke up in the bathtub, covered in ice cubes. On the wall was a note telling me not to move and to call 112 right away. So I did. In the hospital, they told me someone had removed one of my kidneys."

"What did the police say?"

"'They have no clue what they're doing, if you ask me. They say they have never seen this in Denmark before, but what do you expect me to do with that information? I want those who did this to suffer big-time. I want them put away for the rest of their lives. So if anyone knows anything, have them contact me."

The journalist turned and looked into the camera. "And there you have it, Lisa. An angry and frustrated man looking to the public for help. Back to you Lisa."

"Thank you Robert," the anchor took over in the studio. "And Henrik Fenger has put up a reward of 25.000 kroner for anyone who brings him information that can lead to the arrest of the organ thieves."

I was about to shut off the online broadcast, when suddenly the anchor started a new story that caught my interest.

"This just in," she said. "Grave thieves have once again struck in a church. This time it is in Odense Cathedral where they have stolen the remains of Knud den Hellige, former king of Denmark from the year 1080 till 1086. The king was murdered by rebels in Odense in a church where he was kneeling before the altar on July 10th 1086. Last month, the remains of the former king, Erik Kippling, were stolen from Viborg Cathedral. Police are looking to the public for help in this case. More to follow on that story later as it develops during the day."

Then the anchor moved on to another story about the female prime minister who was now in trouble for constantly showing up in public with her expensive Louis Vuitton bag which didn't signal her sympathy for the working class, as she was supposed to, as the leader of the Socialist party.

I turned off the online broadcast and put the iPad down. Julie was in the doorway looking at me. "Coming Mom?"

11

AUGUST 2012

MARTIN DAMSGAARD LOVED BEING on the road. He loved everything about it. He loved meeting new people, he loved staying in new places, new hotels and eating at new restaurants. But most of all, he loved that he could do whatever he pleased without his wife knowing about it.

"So do you come here often?" he said to the girl next to him in the bar. She turned her head and smiled. She had a nice smile, he thought to himself. And her hair was gorgeous. How old was she? Twenty-five? Yeah that was about it. Was she a hooker? He never could tell. Discretely he leaned back in the bar stool and glanced at her from behind.

Nice piece of ass.

She was wearing a very short, tight dress that showed how well-shaped her body was. Martin liked that a lot. He ordered another whiskey and looked at her. "You want another one?" he asked her.

She nodded. "Chardonnay," she said.

"And a Chardonnay for the lovely young lady."

The bartender brought them their drinks and they

sipped them in silence. Martin had picked many women up in bars all over the country, even in Thailand when he went there on business every now and then as well. But this one was better than most he had met. He shook his head and stole a glimpse down her cleavage. Oh how he loved young breasts. Voluptuous and plump. That was the way he preferred them. Martin was a breast man. Lots of his colleagues liked the ass more, but Martin didn't. He liked to take their breasts in his mouth and suck on the nipples, he liked to just feel them between his hands and squeeze them. Oh, he was getting a boner just thinking about it.

His wife Marie had ugly breasts. They were nice back when they first met, but now after they had the three kids, they were flat and hanging and ... well they simply didn't get him excited anymore the way they just dangled there. Martin had told Marie that he would happily pay for her to have them done, but she had refused. Slowly, over the years, the sex had gone from bad to worse to nothing at all. They simply stopped desiring each other. Or at least Martin stopped desiring Marie. He couldn't speak for her or even remotely know what went on in her mind anymore. It seemed that all she did was to yell at him the moment he set foot in the house. So eventually, he did that less and less. He kept coming up with excuses for staying away from the house. Working late, going on a trip, a business meeting downtown that went into a dinner meeting. Stuff like that. And once he finally stepped inside the house, he hurried to the bathroom where he sat for an hour or so reading on his phone or playing Candy Crush, just to avoid Marie and the screaming kids. It had gotten so bad that there were days when he drove into the driveway and stood outside the window of the house looking into the living room, then turned around and decided to go for a drive for a couple of hours, just to avoid them.

The business trips were what kept him going. As a salesman, he travelled all over the world meeting with potential clients and it suited him fine to be almost constantly on the road these days.

"So, you never answered my question," he said.

"What was that?" The woman asked.

"I asked you if you came here often."

The girl smiled again. "I thought it was just a pick-up line."

Martin chuckled. "I guess it was. I'll try something else instead." He leaned over and spoke with a low voice. "So what do I call you when I want to scream out your name during my orgasm?"

The girl chuckled. It was a good sign. Not all girls liked that line. Martin laughed too, then leaned over the bar and drank from his whiskey, imagining going down on the girl next to him.

"You can call me Barbara," she said, licking her teeth.

"Well Barbara," he said tasting her name. "I'm Martin. I have a feeling this is the beginning of a beautiful friendship."

12

AUGUST 2012

BY DINNERTIME, I was starving after playing outside all day with Julie. The weather had been great, so we had played hide and seek in the small forest, then dipped our feet in the lake and looked at all the many fish in the water. After grabbing lunch, we took out a blanket and some books for Julie to read and we laid in the sun talking and reading, me on my iPad, Julie in her books for school. Then Julie suggested we try to walk around the island with our feet in the water. Afterwards, we played soccer on the big lawn until the ball landed in the water and I had to go out and get it in the mushy water.

Now I was looking inside the refrigerator to find the dinner that Peter had told me Mrs. Holm had prepared for us to heat up. I found a roast and potatoes and a brown sauce in a container. I arranged it all on three plates, then put it in the microwave.

Peter came down just in time for dinner with paint on his cheek and fingers.

"Did you have a great time?" I asked curiously and handed him his plate.

He smiled widely. "The best. There is nothing like it. I tell you this is what I want to do with the rest of my life." I guess you can say I have discovered my inner artist. Who would have thought that I had one, huh?"

"I know," I said and served Julie her plate. She dug in immediately and very greedily. Fresh air and playing sure made us both hungry.

I poured some wine for me and Peter and sat down. "I guess we all had a great day, huh?" I said.

Julie nodded with her mouth full. "Mom and I had a lot of fun," she said.

"I'm glad to hear that," Peter said. "I'm so glad to have you both here. I have really missed this. I've missed us."

He looked at me while he spoke. Somehow it made me feel guilty. I was so happy that he was doing better and that we were able to be a family again. It was all I wanted, but at that second, I couldn't help thinking about Sune. I don't know what it was, but somehow I was just reminded of how much I had hurt him. And here I was all happy and with my family again, while he was sitting back there at his apartment in Karrebaeksminde all alone. And it wasn't just guilt, it was something else too. It was a longing. A desire to see him again.

I realized I missed him.

"So, what's up for tomorrow?" Peter asked cheerfully. "Anyone want to go into town?"

"I'd love to," Julie shrieked. "Can we get ice cream at that place again, Dad? Can we? Please?"

Peter laughed. "Of course. That's tradition."

"Just you wait, Mom till you taste this ice cream. It's soooo good. You won't believe it."

"I guess I'll have to then," I said smiling. "You don't have to force me to eat ice cream."

"We have to buy some food too and toilet paper and such," Peter said.

"I thought the good Mrs. Holm took care of all those kinds of things?" I asked sipping my wine. It was a very expensive bottle that Peter had found in the wine cellar below the house. Every sip was like an explosion in my mouth.

"Well she takes care of the more basic stuff. But for the most part, I'm the only one here, so that's easy, but now that there's three of us, I believe it's a little too much to demand of the good old Mrs. Holm."

"Sounds fair. I'd love to see the town," I said and ate a piece of the roast. The good old Mrs. Holm turned out to be quite the cook.

"It's really nice down there, Mommy," Julie said.

Peter chuckled. "It's not much of a town, really. But it has what we need. I need gas for the boat as well."

"There's a hotel down there as well isn't there?" I asked.

"Yes. Hotel Kragen, why?" Peter asked.

"Well there was a story this morning about a guy ..." I paused and looked at Julie, not sure that I wanted her to hear what had happened. "Well something bad happened to him and he was on TV talking about it. I thought about checking the place out."

Peter tilted his head. "And maybe write about it to your newspaper, is that it?" He put his glass down hard on the table. "Christ, Rebekka. Can't you just be on vacation for once?"

"I just wanted to check it out, Peter. That's all."

"Don't you think I know you? It doesn't matter where we go, you're always working."

"Well I'm sorry if I love my job. At least I'm playing with

my daughter when we're on vacation and not hiding in some attic all day."

"Please stop fighting?" Julie said and held both hands to her ears.

Peter sighed and leaned back in his chair. "That was low, Rebekka and you know it."

"Okay, I didn't mean that, but I can't see the big deal about this. All I want is to check the place out, that's all. And so what if I happened to find something interesting to write about? This story is interesting. It's the first case of organ theft in our country. It's important."

"Organ theft?" Julie said. "What's organ theft?"

Peter gesticulated, resignedly. "Now look what you've done. Do you really want your daughter to know about these kinds of things? Do you want her to have bad dreams about organ thieves at night?"

"Of course not," I said.

"It's just because you want your newspaper to have to write the story so you can call your little boyfriend and have him come up here and take pictures for you, isn't it? You want to be with him instead of being here with us? Then go ahead."

Peter got up from the table and left the kitchen slamming the door. I felt so infuriated. Why did I have to ask about that place? Why couldn't I just keep my big mouth shut? Why did he have to be such a prick about it?

"Mom, what is dad talking about? Are Sune and Tobias coming up here?"

"No sweetie. They're not coming. Daddy was just talking nonsense. He didn't mean any of it. Don't worry. Eat your dinner."

"Are you and daddy going to be separated again?"

I smiled and stroked her hair. My beautiful daughter.

The last couple of years had been confusing for her. It was time to give her some stability. If I wanted to be with Peter, then I would have to be more sensitive to his jealousy and make sure I didn't hurt him. "No sweetie. No we're not. We're together now and that's not going to change. You, dad and I love each other very much. But all couples have a fight now and then. That's just the way it is. It'll pass. We'll be friends again soon. Just wait and see."

"So, you'll tell him you're sorry?" She asked.

I looked into her blue eyes and sighed. "I guess I have to, don't I?"

"That's what our teacher tells us to do when we're fighting. The one who says sorry first is the winner."

I laughed out loud. "I guess she's right. At least she's the bigger person, right? The smart one."

"It's smart to say you're sorry," Julie said and finished her food.

I drank my wine thinking about what Peter had said. Why had it infuriated me so much what he had said about Sune? Could it be because he was right?

I shook my head and put the glass down. No it was absurd.

13

AUGUST 2012

THE SEX WAS AMAZING. Martin had never been with anyone this exciting. Not only was she gorgeous, especially without clothes, but her body was so flexible they could do it in positions Martin had only dared to dream about. It was like she was a gift from above, sent to make up for all the bad sex Martin had to live with from his wife.

Or maybe she was sent from the devil. Either way, Martin had the night of his life with this girl and after she left him with a *see you next time you're in town big boy*, Martin fell into a heavy sleep immediately.

He even dreamt about the sex and the girl and in the dream she told him she wanted to stay here with him, that she never wanted to leave him again.

"I think I love you," he whispered out in the darkness, then opened his eyes and realized it was just a dream. Martin closed his eyes again hoping to be able to go back to that warm place of utter happiness, of complete joy that he had been in. He never wanted to leave it again. When he was with her, he didn't think about Marie or the screaming kids. There were no hanging breasts, there was no screaming wife yelling at him for never taking part in anything, for him never being there when he was needed. No there was nothing but him and ... her. Him plunging into her voluptuous breasts, licking her thighs and the silky skin on her stomach that was so flat and not bumpy like Marie's.

Just him and *her*. Just him and Barbara.

Martin looked at the door to the hallway of the hotel and realized she hadn't closed it properly when she left. Secretly, he hoped she would walk in through it again now and they would start all over again, but the door didn't move. He closed his eyes for a second imagining her coming back, telling him she forgot something.

"What did you forget?" he would ask.

"To fuck your brains out again," she would answer. Then they would do it all night long. Over and over again. With her, there would be no cases of not being able to get it up, or closing his eyes and watching a porn-movie on the inside of the eyelids during sex. No with Barbara he didn't have to think about other women or porn, with her it was real. She was so real and his desire for her was very real.

Martin opened his eyes and got out of the bed with the intention of closing the door properly. It was time to get some sleep before he had to move on to another city tomorrow. There had been a lot of driving in his car lately, but he didn't mind. At least he didn't have to go home.

When he shut the door, he thought he heard a sound behind him and turned. He smiled as he walked towards the bathroom where the sound came from. Could it be? Could it really be? Had she come back after all? Had she realized that she enjoyed being with Martin more than with any other man? Did she want more sex or was she going to ask him to take her away from here? Take her with him on his trip around Denmark and stay in hotels, and eat in fancy restaurants. Would he do it? Would he take her?

In a heartbeat.

"Barbara?"

She didn't answer. Martin walked closer to the bathroom, then put his hand on the door and pushed it open. He walked in with a wide smile, thinking he was going to find her in there dressed in sexy underwear, maybe even some of those black stockings that he loved so much. He chuckled at the thought of ripping them off with his teeth.

"I'm coming Barbara."

But what he found in the bathroom wasn't Barbara, much to his surprise. A masked face stared back at him.

"Who are you?" he said with a shivering voice. "What are you doing in my bathroom? Get out of here. I'm trying to sleep."

Before he was able to react, the masked person lifted the arm holding a syringe, planted it in Martin's shoulder and emptied its contents.

"What the hell ...?" he exclaimed and looked at where the needle had gone through the skin. Seconds later, he could no longer move his arms or legs and the last thing he saw before everything went black, was the pink bathroom tiles coming closer and closer.

14

AUGUST 2012

ARIANNA KOSAKOVSKI PULLED HER cart down the hall-way, then pulled out the key that the owner of the hotel had given her. Since there was no sign on the door telling her not to go in, she opened the door and walked in.

As usual, it was with a slight fear of walking in on someone in the room. To think of the things she had seen over the years. The most embarrassing was always when someone was having sex and forgot to put the *do not disturb* sign out on the handle. It happened more than once a month to her and she really hated that. Why people always forgot, she didn't understand. It was so embarrassing for both her and them. Arianna always knocked before entering when she knew the guest hadn't checked out yet and so she did again when walking into room 237 at the Hotel Bellevue in the small town of Hasle.

"Hello? Cleaning?" she said in her bad Danish that still had a heavy Russian accent to it, even after eight years in the country.

There was no answer so Arianna proceeded. She grabbed the clean bed sheets from the cart and walked inside. She picked up the guest's pants from the floor and threw them on a chair before starting to change the bed sheets. People were so messy when they were in hotel rooms. Always leaving their clothes on the floor and even their dirty underwear. Arianna always wore plastic gloves when cleaning the rooms anyway, so she just picked them up, but not without wrinkling her nose in disgust.

Arianna changed the bed sheets and linens first, then brought in the vacuum cleaner and cleaned the floors. When done, she wrapped the cord up and replaced the vacuum cleaner. Outside in the hallway, she greeted her friend Sissel who took care of the rooms on the other side. Sissel smiled and told a dirty joke that made Arianna laugh.

"You're very sick in head, Sissel," she said before she went back inside room 237 carrying towels and new soap for the bathroom. As the door closed behind her, she stopped and looked at the pants that she had put over the back of the chair. She put down the towels and picked up the pants again. She went through the pockets and pulled out a crumpled up one hundred kroner bill. Arianna smiled. It was her lucky day. Often the guests were too drunk to remember what kind of cash they had in their pockets. Especially businessmen travelling alone, picking up women in the bar downstairs who were often hookers. They were way too deep into what was going on to happen to remember putting a crumpled up one hundred kroner bill in their pocket when they left the bar with the girl. They were all thinking with their dicks at that point and would never know it went missing. Arianna straightened the bill out, then put it in her bra. It was Sissel who had taught Arianna how to earn a little extra cash while cleaning the rooms without anyone knowing about it. It was the third time today she had been able to stick a one hundred kroner bill in her bra.

"Just enough for Marius' new shoes," she mumbled happily.

Marius had needed new shoes for a long time now and his father was too cheap to help out.

"I gave you everything, Arianna. All you dreamt of. I married you so you could come to Denmark, I even gave you a child. What else do you want from me?" he often asked.

He was a hopeless alcoholic and Arianna hadn't been able to live with his abuse when he was drunk. Not when it was the boy who had to take the beating. That was too much for her to handle. So, a couple of months ago, she had moved out and asked for separation. The government now said they wanted to throw her out and, for a while now, she had been living with the fear that they would actually do it. Especially since they told her Marius could stay here with his dad. That left Arianna with an impossible choice to make. If Marius stayed, he would get a great education for free and grow up to be a real Dane giving him the best possibilities to amount to something. But she would never see him and he would be with a father who drank and beat him up every now and then. If she took him with her back to Russia, he would grow up in extreme poverty like Arianna had and he wouldn't get much of an education.

Arianna sighed deeply as she picked up the towels and walked towards the bathroom. She tried hard not to think about it since it filled her with deep sadness. She had to cling to that last straw of hope that the government would change its mind and choose not to deport her after all. She had appealed the decision and was now awaiting the final answer.

Arianna felt a chill run down her back as she opened

the door to the bathroom. Not because she was cold, but from the terror that met her in there that, for the first time in a long time, made her forget all about the possibility of deportation. Sitting in the bathtub, almost covered in ice-cubes was the body of a man whom she guessed was the rightful owner of the one hundred kroner bill she was now carrying in her bra.

15

AUGUST 2012

I FOLLOWED Julie's advice and told Peter that I was sorry. It helped, and the next day, after breakfast, we all went to the mainland together in his boat. Julie was talking non-stop about the ice cream and what flavor she was going to get.

I tried hard not to think about the man with the missing kidney. I had even stayed away from my iPad this morning and not read the news. It was, after all, a vacation and no one expected that I would keep myself updated constantly. The problem was just that I loved keeping myself updated. I loved being a part of the stream of news, constantly flowing. It was my life, it was my job and it was a big part of who I was.

Once back on the mainland, we drove to town in Peter's Land Rover. I was looking forward to seeing the small town. The castle on the island was nice and all, but it felt really isolated, like it was very far away from everything.

"I say we grab that ice cream first, before we fill up the car with groceries," Peter said.

"Yay!" Julie shrieked from the backseat.

"Fine with me," I said. I could always eat ice cream, even if it was still morning.

Peter drove the car through a small street with old houses on each side, then past a small movie theater, a couple of stores selling clothes and the grocery store that we were going back to later. He parked the car right in front of the ice cream store. I turned my head to look at Julie, when I spotted Hotel Kragen out the back window. I froze for a second, thinking about the story, then pushed it out of my mind again.

"Come on. Let's go," I said.

Julie jumped out and stormed inside the shop. I grabbed Peter's hand as we followed her inside. The smell was intoxicating. I loved small ice cream shops like this and ordered three scoops in a cone for both Julie and I. Peter only wanted one. Julie and I had whipped cream and chocolate sauce on ours as well. We sat outside at the store's tables and ate greedily, Julie and I getting it smeared all over our faces. Peter looked at me like I was crazy. As usual, he never had anything on his face. *Always the perfectionist.*

"Rebekka," he said. "You've got it all over. Can't you wipe it off or something?"

"Sorry," I said, found a napkin, and wiped it off.

"There is more. Over here," he said and pointed.

I wiped some more and finally got it all off. I ate the rest of the ice cream working really hard on not getting anything on my face and, if I did, I wiped it off right away.

While Julie finished hers, I caught myself staring at the Hotel across the road. I saw photographers outside taking pictures of the facade and journalists with notepads next to them. Even a camera crew from the twenty-four hour news channel TV2News was there. The journalist was interviewing someone outside the building. Peter saw me staring at them and I looked away.

We drove to the grocery store and walked inside. Two women were talking behind the counter. They stopped talking and nodded when we entered, then continued. We took a cart and started filling it. Peter found some wine and steaks, I tried to be good and found a pack of granola.

"You know you're never gonna eat that, Mommy," Julie said. "You always buy granola and then never eat it."

I chuckled. "You're right. Maybe some fresh fruit ... Bananas?"

"I like bananas," Julie said and went to get some.

I couldn't help but eavesdrop on the two women's conversation. It was about what had happened at the Hotel.

"Terrible to wake up like that," one of them said. "Could you imagine? Someone taking your kidney?"

"I heard he had a girlfriend with him," the other said. "A hooker, Arne who works in the bar at the hotel told me she was."

The first woman scoffed. "Well he put it upon himself then didn't he? He had it coming. I heard he had a wife and child."

"Maybe she did it," the second one laughed. "Maybe it was the wife?"

The first one laughed as well. "You bet you that's what I'd do if Hans ever pulled a trick like that on me."

"I bet you would."

Peter approached me with the full cart. "Wow that was fast," I said.

We walked to the counter. The women stopped talking. The one on the right stepped forward and took care of our groceries. She looked at Julie and smiled.

"What a beautiful daughter you have. Are you visiting town?" She asked.

"Yes," I answered.

"You don't live down at the hotel now do you?" She asked, terrified.

I shook my head. "No. No. We live on Dragonsholm. You know, down on the island in the lake."

The woman froze and stared at me. "You're down on the island?"

I nodded. "Yes."

The woman then shook her head and started packing our groceries with fast movements.

"What's wrong?" I asked.

Peter shook his head. "Nothing but superstition," he said. "The locals have always been afraid of the place."

I looked at the woman again. "But why?"

"Nothing good ever came out of that place," the woman said.

"Gerda," the other woman said. "You're scaring the people." She nodded in the direction of Julie as she spoke. Gerda tilted her head and looked at Julie like she felt sorry for her. "Such a beautiful daughter. Such a pretty face."

"Okay," Peter said and took our bags. "I think it's about time we leave now."

In the car on our way back, I couldn't stop thinking about what the women had said. Peter saw it on my face. "Nothing but superstition," he said.

"I know. But ... well, you know me. I really wanted to know the story. It sounded like they knew a good story."

Peter rolled his eyes. "You're impossible. It's nothing but rumors and old wives' tales. An old castle like this one will always have its share of ghost stories, like the one with the carriage that you hear at night that is supposed to be the carriage taking the Earl's body away."

"I think I heard it," Julie said. "One night I heard it."

Peter looked in the rearview mirror. "Nonsense," he said. "It's just your mind playing tricks on you, making you think you hear it because I told you the story. See that's how stories like this work. You believe them and then you think you hear or see it and then you're scared. It's all in your mind like all other superstitions."

"Do you know them?" I asked. "Do you know the stories?"

Peter exhaled. "I know some of them, parts of them, yes. But do you really want to scare your daughter further? I could also go online and find some scary ghost stories to give her nightmares. Is it really worth it?"

I shrugged and looked out the window. "No. You're probably right. I was just curious."

"Oh come on Daddy, tell us just one of them, please? I promise I won't get nightmares," Julie said.

"Well, all I know is that they say some doctor once went amok back when it was a mental institution. Apparently he killed some patients or something. Okay, not just some, but a lot of patients, according to the story."

"How?" Julie asked. "How did he kill them?"

"He performed operations as experiments. One of them being him removing their organs one at a time, thinking sickness in the organs caused them to be deranged. In the end, the patients naturally died. That's all. Nothing but a crazy doctor. Now I think we should find something nice to talk about. How about that ice cream, huh? It was truly something."

16

JULY 1999

VALDEMAR WAS GROWING SO FAST NOW, Anna could hardly keep up. Every day he seemed to have new victories and to conquer the impossible. Only four years old and he was talking like a ten year old, the doctor had told her. His mind seemed to be a masterpiece of its own. He had taught himself to do many things that Anna never thought he would be able to do. And, often, the solution was among the simplest. He got by doing a lot of things with his toes and feet. One day when Anna was in the living room, Valdemar called her from the kitchen and asked her to come and see something. As she entered, she was stunned to realize that her little boy had managed to tie one of his father's ties around the refrigerator handle and fasten it with a knot using his toes. Then, he put the end of it on his shoulder and, using his mouth, started pulling till the door opened.

"There," he said. "Now I can get my own food."

Anna laughed and picked him up. Then she danced while holding him tight. Valdemar laughed and laughed. After that day, he didn't stop amazing his mother with his accomplishments. He used his chin to hold his plate between the chin and the shoulder and carry it to the table when it was dinnertime. He pressed buttons on the microwave with his nose and he played videogames by simply using his toes.

Anna was thrilled to see how many things he was capable of and, as the days went by, her hopes rose that he would one day be able to take care of himself.

But what broke her heart was seeing him making all this progress and then looking at his dad for acknowledgement and never receiving it. Every day, Anna told Michael about what Valdemar did now and how clever he was, but every day he would answer the same: "The kid is a loser. He will never be able to do anything."

And every time he said that, he broke Anna's heart a little. Especially when Michael would look at Valdemar with resentment at the dinner table when he ate either by simply sticking his face into the plate or when Anna fed him with the spoon.

"See?" he said. "He still can't even eat on his own."

Every day, Anna saw how the hurt grew in Valdemar's eyes and she cursed her husband for not seeing the progress, for not hoping and dreaming of a future for their son like she did. Then one day, when Valdemar was four, he was occupied in the garage for a long time and Anna was worried. Valdemar loved hanging out in there, using his dad's tools when he wasn't at home, with nothing but his feet. Anna was wondering what he was up to when he suddenly stormed into the kitchen holding something between his chin and shoulder. He placed it on the table, but still Anna couldn't see what it was. It looked like a small iron pipe that he had welded onto a small round slice of metal that could turn. Anna couldn't really see what it was, but Valdemar soon showed her. He smiled like this was the proudest moment of his life. Anna didn't understand.

"How did you make this?"

"I welded it."

"You used your dad's welder? Are you insane? You could get hurt!" Anna was furious. Just the thought of him alone with that dangerous instrument made her heart race. Didn't he understand that he wasn't like other kids? Didn't he know he was handicapped? It was like he refused to accept the fact that everything was harder for him than for other kids.

"I put on dad's helmet. Don't worry, Mommy. Let me show you what this is for. Just wait and see. You'll love it. Grab a spoon," he said.

Anna handed him a spoon.

"And a bowl of cereal."

"But it's almost time for dinner," she argued. "I don't want you filling up on all kinds of food before we eat. Daddy will be home any minute now."

"Mommy. Just help me, will you please?"

Anna sighed and poured some cornflakes into a bowl and poured milk on top of them. Then, she placed it in front of Valdemar.

Valdemar picked up the spoon using his mouth, put it in the bowl, and dug up a spoonful of cereal. Still using his mouth, he placed it on top of the iron pipe that had a small submersion through the center where the handle of the spoon fitted perfectly. Then using his nose, Valdemar pushed the spoon around till he could reach the food on the end of it and ate it.

Valdemar looked up with a big smile. Anna burst into tears just as the door opened and Michael stepped in.

"What's going on here?" he asked. "Why are you crying?"

"Oh Michael. You've got to see this," Anna said and ran to him. "Our boy has taught himself how to eat with a spoon. Come and see."

Anna noticed Valdemar's body was shaking as he picked up the spoon with his mouth again. He managed to get cereal on it, then placed it in the submersion again and turned it with his nose. Then he opened his mouth to eat the food from the end of the spoon, when his nose accidentally tipped the spoon off the iron pipe and it fell down on the table spreading cereal and milk on the newspaper lying next to his bowl.

Valdemar looked up at his dad who growled and picked up the paper and started to walk away.

"It worked just fine before," Anna said. "It really did Michael. He was eating on his own. I tell you it's a miracle."

Michael turned around and looked at Anna. "A miracle? You call that a miracle? I call it a failure. A pathetic failure. So what if he can learn how to eat on his own? Most kids can do that when they're less than a year. How is he ever going to ride a bike?"

17

AUGUST 2012

AT THE HOSPITAL, THE piggy-doctor told Henrik that he was fine and ready to be discharged.

"We would like for you to come back for a check-up to make sure your remaining kidney is working properly in about two weeks. Until then you must rest, give your body time to heal. And for God's sake, try not to get yourself too agitated."

Henrik growled and gathered his belongings. He looked at the display on the cellphone while waiting for the taxi in the hospital lobby. No one had tried to call him. Henrik's stomach hurt and he found the pills the doctor had given him for the pain. He swallowed one without water and stared once again at the phone.

Why hadn't she called? Why hadn't Janni answered her phone when he had tried to call her? She was, after all, his wife. She had to know that he was in the hospital for Pete's sake. The police said they had informed her. Where was she?

The taxi drove up in front of the entrance and Henrik got up from the chair and walked towards it, taking slow steps to ease the pain. He was sweating heavily. The taxi driver held the door for him and took his suitcase. Henrik growled when he noticed how the taxi-driver handled his suitcase, banging it around, not caring that he was making scratches and bumps in it. Henrik shook his head and took in a deep breath.

Probably Pakistani with that turban on his head. Probably a terrorist in training. Just like the rest of them. Nothing but trouble.

Henrik shook his head while the man smiled at him, showing a row of pearly white teeth in his brown face.

Why does the Danish population refuse to see that all those people only come here to destroy our nation from the inside? First they will be elected for parliament, then they will build their ugly, noisy mosques and make us stop having Christmas because it is offensive to them and soon no one will eat pork anymore and the brown-skinned will be in charge. That is what is going to happen and it has already started, hasn't it? They are already complaining about the Christmas trees and the pork served in schools. And the Danes are stupid enough to listen and then they change it in order to not offend the growing Muslim community. Meanwhile, they have their meetings where they declare death to the Danish population behind our backs. It should be illegal to be this freaking stupid!

"So where are we going?" the brown-skinned man with the turban asked. The taxi didn't smell as bad as Henrik had expected it to.

Henrik looked at his phone and felt the anger rise inside of him again. He wanted to crush the phone between his fingers.

Home? Are you going home? Back to Roskilde and a woman who doesn't care about you?

"Where to?" the taxi-driver asked again.

His calmness irritated Henrik. *Probably Buddhist or something stupid.* Henrik felt like screaming. He restrained himself and made a decision.

"Take me back to Brabrand. To Hotel Kragen. I have some unfinished business there."

"As you wish," the taxi driver said and started the car.

Henrik found his wife in the contact information on his phone and looked at it. Should he text her? Let her know he was out of the hospital? Nah, she didn't even care that he was in there in the first place, did she? No she would have visited or at least called. Henrik looked at the photo on his phone showing his wife and son. Didn't he mean anything to them?

As the taxi drove out of Aarhus and into the country-side, Henrik opened Facebook. There were a ton of messages for him on his wall from colleagues and acquaintances wishing him well and telling him they saw him on TV and how awful it was what had happened to him. Most of them told him to let them know if there was *anything they could do for him.*

"Bah," Henrik said out loud. It was so easy to show sympathy on Facebook without meaning anything by it.

Henrik found his wife's Facebook page and scrolled on her wall, reading all the messages and updates. On the day he had been admitted to the hospital, she had changed her status from married to *single.* Her status today was a quote from one of her favorite TV shows, *Sex and the City.* *"Men cheat for the same reason that dogs lick their balls ... because they can."*

Henrik felt infuriated and threw the phone on the seat next to him with a groan. The taxi driver looked at him in the rearview mirror.

"Everything all right?" He said with his stupid foreign accent that made Henrik even angrier.

"Yes, everything is all right," he said imitating him rolling on the r like he had done.

So she had guessed that he was with a woman that night. *Big deal.*

The taxi came to a stop and Henrik paid the man and got out. With much discomfort, he walked inside the lobby. Luckily, there were no journalists there. Henrik had feared they would still be there, but they had probably moved on. The man behind the counter gasped when he recognized Henrik's face.

"Let me get the owner on the phone," he said.

"No. No. I'm not here to talk to the owner. I need to talk to someone in the bar. Could you help me find who the bartender was that night?"

"S ... ssure," the clerk stuttered. "That would be Arne. Let me find him for you. One moment, please."

Henrik nodded and held on to the counter. At the hospital, they had told him he would experience pain for the next couple of days, but it was perfectly normal. There was nothing about this pain that seemed normal to Henrik. He sighed and looked around. Eyes were watching him, scrutinizing him, and when he turned to look at them, they looked away. *So I'm the freak now, huh? I'm the freaking talk of this small town?*

"Here is the gentleman who wishes to speak to you."

Henrik heard the voice behind him and turned around. A man, whom he recognized as the bartender who had waited on them that night, looked back at him. He reached out his hand. "I'm so sorry, sir. For what happened that night."

"Good," Henrik said. He closed his eyes as a wave of

pain rolled in over him.

"Are you alright sir? Should we call for help?"

"No. No. No help please. I'm fine. The doctor at the hospital said it was perfectly normal to have some pain. Besides, I don't care. I just want to find whoever did this to me."

"At least sit down, sir," the clerk said and helped Henrik to a chair.

"Don't fuss around me," Henrik growled and removed the clerk's hand from his arm. The way he held him made him feel like an old man or a cripple. And no one treated him like a cripple. Henrik was a man at his best age. He was many things. He was handsome, he was charming and had a way with the ladies, but he wasn't pathetic. He didn't need people's help. "I hate fussing."

The clerk stepped back. "Sorry, sir. I didn't mean to ..."

"Well, you did." Henrik sat in the chair. It felt good to rest a little. He looked up at the bartender. "I want to know who she was," he said. "I want to know everything you know about the girl."

"Very well sir. But I do believe I told everything to the police."

Henrik looked into the bartender's eyes. So that's how Janni knew. The police had told her? Asked her if she knew? Had they no respect for people's privacy?

Henrik's hands were shaking in anger. The clerk and bartender saw it on his face. There was no way this girl was going to get away with ruining his life like this. Once he found her, she was getting what she had coming to her.

And it wasn't going to be pretty.

Henrik looked at the bartender. "What have you got? I need to know everything. If you give me what I need, I'll consider not pressing charges against the hotel."

18

AUGUST 2012

THE NEXT MORNING AFTER BREAKFAST, my phone rang while I was doing a puzzle on the floor with Julie. The display told me it was my editor Jens-Ole. I got up and walked out of the room before I picked it up.

"Rebekka," I said.

"I know you're on vacation, I know you need time with your family to get your marriage fixed and all that. Believe me, I know that and I have tried everything to find another solution, but the thing is ... we need you," Jens-Ole said. "Desperately."

I would be lying if I said there wasn't a part of me that was happy to hear I was needed. I loved my work and I loved that I was so good at it.

"You're still in Brabrand, right?"

"Yes."

"You've heard about the guy who had his kidney stolen, right?" Jens-Ole asked.

"Sure did."

"Did you hear about the second guy?"

My heart dropped. There had been a second one? "No.

I have been trying to stay out of it ... it doesn't matter. What happened?"

"Same story. Guy at a hotel is attacked at night, cleaning lady finds him next morning, dead in the bathtub, missing his liver. It's gone, someone had removed it while he was sedated, according to the police."

"But he was killed? The first guy survived, right?"

"Yeah they only took his kidney. You have two of those, but only one liver. In both cases, they had their bodies covered in ice cubes. Police say they are certain they're looking for the same guy. Someone who knows a lot about surgery. They say the cuts are very professionally made with a scalpel and all the right equipment and all."

"Creepy. So the person they're looking for might be a doctor?" I asked. There was something about this story that gave me the chills. The thought of people being sedated and having their organs stolen without their knowledge freaked me out.

"Maybe. Someone with expertise in the area at least."

"So what do you want from me?" I asked.

"The second case was close to where you're at too. It was in Hasle. That's only about ten minutes by car from where you're staying, I think. Hotel Bellevue."

"So what is it you want me to do?" I asked, thinking I had no idea how to tell Peter about this without him getting angry. He never understood having a career, providing for your family. He came from a very rich background and always had the money he needed for anything. He never had to actually work for a living. Not that I ever envied him his childhood and upbringing that, for the most part, took place at a boarding school away from his parents. But still. He never wanted to make a career for himself since there was no reason to do so. I had to do my best, always, or I was out. A journalist was never better than her last story. It was as simple as that.

"I want you to go to Hasle and make a report from there. Talk to the people working there, preferably the cleaning lady who found the body. Talk to people around, in the streets or whatever and find out if they're scared. Try to figure out what the police are doing about this. Could it be a gang of some sort? Eastern Europeans stealing our organs at night and selling them on the black Russian market? What? What are we talking about here? Could they do this anywhere? In people's private homes? We have had many cases of home invasions where Eastern Europeans break into houses in the middle of the night and beat people up with baseball bats, killing people for only a couple of hundred kroner. Are they going to take their organs next? Is it a new trend in organized crime that we should be afraid of? What are they doing about it? I don't want to wake up one morning having something missing from inside of me."

"Okay, okay. I get the picture." I said.

"That's my girl. We need this. We're the only newspaper not writing anything about this story. It's embarrassing. The bosses are mad at me. They want you on this story. You're our best man, or woman. If you do it, I'll even throw in an extra week of vacation. Take any week off this fall. Be with your family then. I promise I won't disturb you this time. I'll throw away your number. Just give me my story."

"Got it," I said.

"Great. By the way I have informed Sune and he's on his way. He'll meet you in Hasle."

19

AUGUST 2012

THOMAS DE QUINCEY WAS typing on his laptop with a grin. Bill Durgin had struck again and the story was all over the media now. And even better, this time Bill had actually killed his victim, just like Thomas had wanted him to. Removing an organ and letting the victim survive was fun, yes, but very risky. Bill had wanted to just remove a part of the liver, since the liver then would regenerate itself as it did in people donating parts of their liver to a family member who needed a new liver. But Thomas had put his foot down. He wanted Bill to move on, to make his first kill. And he had succeeded.

I removed it all as you told me to. He died slowly, Bill wrote.

Excellent. You did well, Thomas wrote. *How did it feel?*

Better than expected. I think I actually enjoyed it a little. He deserved what he got, the bastard.

Wonderful. Now you have taken it to the next step. The first kill is always the hardest, but also the sweetest. From now on, you'll have no trouble killing again, Thomas wrote.

What about your contribution? Have you given it more thought?

I have and he's yours, Bill wrote without hesitating. It pleased Thomas immensely. There was nothing better than obedient followers.

Oh how pleased I am to hear that. There is nothing like the first kill that should be savored and remembered. I'll make sure to immortalize what you have done. Your master-piece is safe with me.

What do I need to do? Bill wrote.

Nothing. I'll send my guy to pick him up. Don't worry. I'll take care of everything. Just you worry about your next move. You need to strike while the iron is hot. The entire country is looking at you and focusing on your art right now. This is your moment ... your fifteen minutes of fame. Enjoy it.

I will.

Thomas logged off, then closed the lid of the computer and clapped his hands with joy. He looked at himself in the mirror hanging on the wall.

"You're a genius, Thomas."

He smiled at his own reflection. This last couple of months had been so exciting, he could barely keep it inside. He wanted to scream and yell and laugh. He could hardly believe his life's work was almost done. His masterpiece was almost ready for the world to see. It was a dream that came true. The work of a genius. That's what they would all say, wasn't it? He was going to write himself into the history books. Future generations would hear about him in school and his name would be whispered in the darkness of the night when children told their scary stories. He would be a myth, a legend. And people would fear his name like they feared Jack the Ripper or Ted Bundy. Oh, but he would be so much bigger than them.

"But it's not time to celebrate yet," he told his own reflection. "Your work is not done." Thomas shook his head.

No, he was still missing the most vital part of all. The last and most important part. The part he desired the most for personal reasons. The final revenge over the woman who broke his heart. No not just broke it, tore it apart, ripped it from his chest and stepped on it afterwards.

His last and final piece was the body of Rebekka Franck.

Thomas smiled widely again. This time he was going to succeed. This time there was nothing in the way. Using Allan Witt had been a bad idea, and Thomas was actually happy that it hadn't succeeded. It was unfulfilling to have someone else do it for you, when it's your revenge, when it's you who want to do it.

Thomas gritted his teeth thinking about her. He clenched his fist and hit it into the wall behind the mirror. Then he laughed manically. He turned and grabbed the camera on the counter. He had it all planned out. With the camera, he was going to document his actions. He was going to take a picture every minute until she drew her last and final breath. Documenting the pain he inflicted upon her, documenting the distress a person experienced right before she died. It had never been done before. It was perfect. The work of a true artist, they would say.

An artist willing to go all the way for his art.

20

AUGUST 2012

I SAT WITH THE phone in my hand for a little while after hanging up, not knowing how to handle this. Then I decided to just do it. I walked back in with Julie.

"Work?" she asked.

I smiled. "You know me a little too well, don't you?"

She shrugged. "It's okay, Mommy. I know you love your job."

I stared at my daughter. My beautiful and suddenly so very grown-up daughter. I kneeled next to her and hugged her. "My boss is giving me another week off instead of the days I'm spending on this, and I thought that maybe I'll take it when you have your fall break in October. Maybe we could go somewhere far away where they can't get a hold of me and make me work. Maybe we'll go to Spain or France? What do you say?"

Julie looked up at me. "That sounds really nice, Mommy. I'd like that. Maybe Tobias could come as well?"

I froze. "Tobias?"

"Yes. I really miss him. Don't you miss Sune?"

Children and their bluntness. Just bursting it all out

without thinking. Just saying what everybody else is thinking or won't admit they're thinking. I nodded. "Yes, sweetie. I miss him."

"Good," she said.

"I thought you liked that mommy was back with daddy?" I asked.

"I do. I love it Mommy. But I liked Sune too. And I looove Tobias. You know that. We're going to get married. We already planned that."

"Wow that was early."

"Yeah, but first I have to finish college. Tobias wants to be an astronaut, so he needs to get a space education first and that takes a long time, I think. He won't be home much since he'll be flying out in space a lot, but I can take care of the kids. We might fight a little over him always being away, but we'll make it work. I'll have my clinic at my house so I can be home a lot."

"Your clinic? What kind of clinic is that?" I asked trying hard not to laugh.

"My dog hospital, of course. I'll be a vet. But only for dogs. I don't like cats. Maybe I'll treat a tiger if they bring him to me. But only baby tigers since they're not scary. They are really cute."

I chuckled. "Boy you have you entire life all figured out, don't you?"

"Yes, Mommy." Julie looked deep into my eyes. "You should figure your life out too."

I looked at her, astonished and slightly surprised as well. *From children and drunk people you hear the truth,* was a Danish saying. Was that what this was? Her speaking the truth I refused to admit to myself?

The door opened and Peter entered. "What do you guys

say we have some lunch?" he asked. I looked at him. He froze when our eyes met.

"Mommy's going to work," Julie said.

Peter sighed. "Really?"

"Yeah, I'm sorry. They just called. They need me to do the story about the kidney-guy. There has been another case in Hasle not far from here. Also in a hotel. They want me to cover the story. I'm sorry. They gave me another week off this fall instead. I thought maybe we could ..."

Peter lifted his hand and stopped me. "And I guess that photographer boyfriend of yours is going too, am I right?"

"Peter. Don't start ... This is my job. This is what it is like to be a journalist. You have to be available when they need you, when a story breaks. That's just the way it is. If they can't count on me, they'll let me go. I'll never get the career I want."

"Then don't," Peter said.

"I can't just forget all about my career. I have bills to pay, I have a daughter to provide for."

"Not if you're with me. I can provide for the both of you, you know that as well as I do."

"You know that is not what I want."

"What? To be a family?"

"Come on. That's not fair."

"Why not? If you gave up that so-called career of yours, you could stay home and be a mother and a wife and I would support all of us. We could travel all over the world if that was what you wanted. I'd give you everything."

I exhaled and shook my head. "Yes Peter I do believe you'd give me the world. I know you'd give me anything money could buy. But money doesn't buy happiness. And working makes me happy. Like it or not, I'm going."

I grabbed my bag and put my iPad in it along with my

notepad and phone. Then I took my jacket from the closet in the hall. I kissed Julie and held her tight.

"It's okay, Mommy. It really is." Then she whispered in my ear. "Can't wait for Spain."

Peter followed me to the door. I turned and looked at him. I stroked his cheek gently. He hadn't shaved since we got there. Stubble looked great on him. His hair was getting gray on the sides.

"I'm sorry," I whispered. "I'll be back tonight."

Peter sighed and held on to my wrist, then kissed it. He leaned over and kissed my lips. The warmth from his kiss made me almost regret I was going.

"See you later," he said.

21

SEPTEMBER 2001

SHE BOUGHT HIM A BIKE. He had been asking for one ever since he was four and his dad asked the question:

How will he ever ride a bike?

It had tormented Valdemar ever since and his mother knew that, but up until this day she had refused to buy him a bike just because he wanted to impress his dad. The fact was, it was impossible for the boy to ride a bike and it was way too dangerous. He would only get hurt and his dad would be less impressed than ever.

It was a bad idea.

At least that was what she thought until the day she finally gave in to the boy's pressure. Every afternoon when they walked home from school, Valdemar would stop in front of the bicycle store and glare at the many bikes. There was one, especially, that held his attention. It was blue, sparkling blue with a wide seat and, most importantly of all, it looked exactly like the other kids' bikes. It wasn't made for handicapped boys. It wasn't different.

So one afternoon, Anna finally gave in to those big,

pleading eyes. She bought the bike while the storeowner looked at her strangely.

"He won't be able to ride it, you know," he said.

Anna looked at the boy who refused to listen to sayings like these. The same boy who had taught himself to use a spoon, who had rebuilt their house by adding things everywhere so he wouldn't need anyone's help with anything, the boy whose life up until now had been a study in engineering.

Then she smiled. "Oh, he will," she said. "He'll find a way."

"Suit yourself," the storeowner said.

Never had Anna seen her boy as proud as when they brought it home and she placed it in the garage where Valdemar wanted it. Now he was working on something in there that he didn't want her to see until it was done, he told her and she was waiting in the living room, biting her nails, wondering what he had come up with. Worrying that his dad would be angry or let him down once again.

Michael stayed away from the house more and more. Often a week would pass by where they didn't see him. He was on the road, working, meeting clients he told her if she asked. But the trips were getting more and more often now and Anna started wondering what he was doing all this time. Staying in hotels? Eating alone in restaurants? It was no secret he didn't enjoy being at home anymore. He hadn't enjoyed it ever since Valdemar was born.

Anna sighed and hid her face in her hands. She missed him so much. For six years now she had been on her own with this. She had been alone, abandoned, having to make all the decisions herself, and raising Valdemar on her own trying hard to protect him from getting hurt by his father's resentment towards him. It was heartbreaking and wore on her strength. The constant worrying about her boy had made her old. Her body was skinny, her breasts hanging. Her hair had turned white overnight, right before Valdemar's first birthday. It was the constant worrying, the doctor said. It happened from time to time.

"At least you won't have to worry about the greys popping up one after another like most people," he had told her to cheer her up.

"But I look like an old woman. At the age of thirty?"

"I think you're beautiful," the doctor had told her and Anna had blushed. It had been a long time since anyone had told her she was beautiful.

While waiting in the living room for whatever wonder her boy had now come up with, she grabbed her long white hair and looked at it. It wasn't too bad. At least she had learned to live with it, just as she had learned to live with the fact that her husband was never going to accept their son and his handicap. He saw it as a failure, like she had failed him as a wife for giving him a son with no arms.

"If only he could see what I see," she mumbled, as she heard the door to the garage open and Valdemar call for her to come.

22

AUGUST 2012

I TOOK PETER'S BOAT and sailed to the shore where I borrowed Peter's Land Rover to go to Hasle. I didn't enjoy the fact that I left Peter and Julie alone on the island. There was an old fishing boat in the yard they could use to get to the main land if they really needed it, but still, I felt like I was cutting off their only connection to the world outside the island.

"They'll be fine," I mumbled and checked my hair in the rearview-mirror. I parked the Land Rover across the street from the Hotel Bellevue. The street was packed with cars and photographers; camera crews were crowding outside the building. I drew in a deep breath and looked at my phone. I had received a text from Sune.

MEET YOU AT THE FRONT ENTRANCE

I looked at it again with my heart pounding in my chest. Was I ready for this? Was I ready to face him again? I put the phone in my bag and decided I was.

I walked up towards the crowd of working journalists and photographers. A journalist from TV2 News was in the middle of a live broadcast, speaking into the camera.

"... while they said after the first incident in Brabrand, they were certain this was nothing but a one-time incident, the police are now wondering if there is actually an organized gang behind these attacks. They are asking the public for help, since the killer left no fingerprints or any trace behind. Back to you Lisa."

I snuck past her and into the crowd. I elbowed my way, ducked under cameras to not be seen until I spotted him. As usual, he stuck out in the crowd like no one else. Tall and skinny and the only one here with a Mohawk.

My heart dropped. We had spent so much time together over the last several years. So many great articles, so much fun with our kids, so much love between us. Could I just throw that away? And for what? Pursuing some happiness and family life that I didn't even know if I wanted after all?

Julie was right. I needed to figure out my life soon.

I exhaled and walked closer. Sune was already taking pictures. I put my hand on his shoulder. He turned around and our eyes met. For one moment, we both forgot everything. It felt like a punch in my stomach. It completely knocked the air out of me. At that instant, looking into his eyes, seeing him so close to me again, I felt heartbroken. Heartbroken with longing for feeling his arms around me again. Heartbroken for wanting so badly to kiss those lips again. And, worst of all, I sensed he felt it too. He stared at me like he was searching for words, looking for something smart to say, to break this moment between us. I watched his lips part, but no sound came out. All the people around us became nothing but a distant buzz.

Speak for crying out loud. Say something.

It was Sune who said the first word. "Hi."

I smiled. "Hi."

He bit his lip, then lowered his eyes. And just like that,

the moment was gone. "Let's get to work," he said. "What do you need?"

"I ... uh ... I was thinking some pix of the main building. The front entrance, maybe even all the journalists in front of it to document how big of a story it is."

"Already got all that."

"Great."

I cleared my throat. I felt like crying. Being this close to him again reminded me of everything we had together. Of all that I had given up to save my marriage. I felt sick to my stomach with longing for him. I pushed it away. I swallowed my tears and my emotions along with them.

"What's next?" he asked.

"Let's get out of this crowd. We're not getting anything here that all the others won't have."

"I hear you."

We elbowed our way out and walked around the building. "I want to talk to the employees," I said.

Sune followed me. How I loathed this strange air between us. Why couldn't we just go back to how things were? Why did everything have to change all of a sudden? I hated it.

We walked around a corner and bingo. Three people who looked like hotel employees were smoking behind the dumpsters. I turned and winked at Sune.

"There is our story."

23

AUGUST 2012

THE BARTENDER HAD SEEN the girl often at the bar, he told Henrik. She came there to pick up guys and he thought she was a prostitute, but she could just be a girl looking for men. It was hard to tell. Whatever name she had given to Henrik the night they had spent together, he couldn't remember it, no matter how hard he tried. But the bartender knew it.

Annabelle Svendsen.

After getting her name it didn't take Henrik long to look her up. There were only two people by that name in all of Denmark. And one of them lived in Elsinore, in the other end of the country. But one lived in Silkeborg, half an hour's drive from Brabrand.

Henrik called the police from the car he had rented on his way there and spoke to officer Jansson, asking him how the investigation was going. The officer told him they were very busy, but they would let him know as soon as they knew anything. Henrik considered asking about the girl, about why they hadn't arrested Annabelle, but that would be the same as admitting that he had lied when he said he slept alone that night.

"So, there are no suspects yet?" he asked. "No arrests made?"

"No. None so far. We'll let you know, Mr. Fenger."

"Fucking morons," Henrik groaned as he hung up. Why hadn't they arrested the girl? Well, it was all the same. He was actually glad they hadn't. Or else he wouldn't get his revenge, now would he? In his head, the story was as clear as they get. He had offended the girl, she was angry with him because he didn't want to be her boyfriend, because he didn't want to take her out to fancy vegetarian restaurants and chitchat about beetroot and zumba-classes.

But why she had chosen to take his kidney? Henrik had no answer to that question. Maybe it was just her way of getting back at him, the freaking cunt. Maybe it was bigger than that. Maybe she was even making money off of his kidney, earning a living on selling his organ. Henrik didn't care what the motive or purpose was. All he knew was that he wanted to see her in pain for what she had done. Unlike the police, he wasn't going to let her get away with it.

Henrik slammed his fist into the wheel of the car several times in anger, then drove off towards Silkeborg.

Annabelle Svendsen lived in an apartment close to the center of town. Henrik found a parking space a block or so away and walked the rest of the way so he wouldn't be seen. As he stood in front of the front door to the apartment building, he wondered how to get inside. He considered just pushing all the buttons to all the apartments until someone thought he was the paperboy and buzzed him inside, when suddenly someone, a young girl, walked out of the door. He smiled at her and grabbed the door before it shut.

"Thanks," he said.

The young girl smiled, then disappeared down the street. Henrik walked up the stairs, checking every nametag on the doors on the way up. On the third floor, he found her name.

A.Svendsen

Henrik chuckled. It was almost too easy. It was like the universe wanted him to find her. He lifted his hand and put his finger on the doorbell. Then he waited. Henrik fixed his hair and put on his most devilish smile.

The door opened. The girl looked at him with astonishment.

"You?"

"Me."

"But ... What are you doing here?"

"We need to talk."

"Sure." Annabelle stepped aside. "Come on in."

Henrik smiled widely, then walked past her into her apartment. Annabelle closed the door behind him.

"I'll make us some coffee," she said.

24

AUGUST 2012

"Listen to this sentence. *The first thing I saw was his arm. When I walked inside the bathroom, his arm was sticking out from above the bathtub."*

I looked at Sune who was as thrilled as I was. We were sitting in the back seat of Peter's Land Rover, each with our laptops on our laps. I was writing my article and Sune was uploading pictures.

"Look at this," he said and turned the screen. "Look at the dread in her eyes. You can just feel how freaked out she is."

"That is a beautiful picture," I said. "Perfect for the story."

We had landed a scoop. Nothing less. The three men smoking behind the dumpsters had helped us find the cleaning lady who had first discovered the body and she was willing to talk to us in her apartment, not far from the hotel. We were the only ones to find her and get the interview. She had even given me a new story that I wanted to write next week when I got back to work. She was about to be thrown out of the country just because she had left her abusive husband. I promised to run her story and maybe try and wake up the politicians.

Now I was writing all she had told me about finding the body in my article. When I was done with that, I wrote another article about the police and how they had no clue in this case. I had spoken to them earlier on the phone and gotten the latest details for my articles.

"How about this one?" Sune asked and showed me another picture of the girl that he had taken while she was talking to me.

"I love the way she is covering her mouth with her hand," I said.

"It's perfect too," he said.

I looked at him and smiled. This felt good. I had forgotten how much I enjoyed working with Sune. He was the only one who always understood where I wanted to go with a story, what kind of emotions I wanted to evoke in people reading it. And his pictures always matched what I was going for.

Jens-Ole freaked out when he heard we had the girl. "I knew you two would deliver," he yelled. "I knew it. I just knew it."

I chuckled and put him on speakerphone so Sune could listen in as well. "The articles are almost done. There is one about what the police are doing as well. Just a small one, since they're screwed on this one. They have no idea where to turn, how to deal with this."

"That's what I thought," Jens-Ole said. "Everybody's doing the police-angle and the possible Eastern European angle, so we're not going to do much of that. I like the personal touch to our stories. I'd like more of that."

"Well now you have this one. It's really good. She was

very honest and brutally detailed. You better read it to make sure it's not too much."

"I don't see how it could be," Jens-Ole said.

"Do it anyway, alright?" I said. "I don't want any complaints afterwards."

"I will. Don't worry. Oh ... by the way?"

I closed my eyes. I knew that sentence. He had more for us. "Yes? You want something else too, don't you?"

"Well just one more thing."

"It seems there is always just one more thing," I said, but I didn't feel angry about it. I was happy to be on a story again. I was thrilled to be out on the road and mostly I was enjoying spending time with Sune again. Working on a story gave me the right to be with him without feeling guilty about it. Not too guilty at least.

"Sara, the sweetheart, has been working hard on this all day and she finally succeeded this afternoon. You can't say no to this."

"Let's see about that," I said, wondering about Peter and how he was going to take it. "What've you got?"

"Sara found the kidney-guy. She spoke to him earlier on the phone and he agreed to do a solo interview. You know, details about what happened and what it felt like to wake up missing a part of you and all that. So far, he has only done that one short TV interview on the first day in the hospital. Since then, he has refused to talk to any media."

"Until now, huh?"

"It's a scoop. He hasn't done any longer interviews. This is yours."

I looked at Sune who was nodding eagerly.

"Don't think we'll pass on that one," I said.

"Great. Wonderful. It's in Silkeborg. You might have to spend the night there. He has agreed to do it late tonight.

He's staying there, but only tonight, he said. He'll go back to Roskilde tomorrow."

"Ah, he's from Roskilde on Zeeland. Makes it an even better story for Zeeland Times."

"It sure does. Meet him at the lobby of Hotel Mercury at nine tonight."

"We'll be there."

AUGUST 2012

"So ... how are you?" Annabelle asked, looking truly concerned.

What an actress.

Henrik could play a game too. He smiled and tilted his head. "Never better," he said.

"But ...But I thought you ... I mean I saw you on TV. They said you ..." Annabelle looked down like she didn't want to say it out loud.

Nicely played. Making me believe you're all innocent and scared by my story. Very nice. Done a lot of acting before, have we?

"Ah that. Well, at least I have two kidneys right?" Henrik laughed manically and grabbed a Danish butter-cookie that Annabelle had put on the table in front of him.

"It must have been really scary walking up like that?" She asked sounding concerned.

I'm not buying it, bitch. Too forced. Too much.

"Oh yes it was. It certainly was a frightening experience. What was it the police called it? Oh yes. Unfortunate. An unfortunate experience it was." Henrik took another cookie and chewed it with his mouth open just to annoy her.

"But you're alright now? I mean they let you out of the hospital?"

"Except for the fact that I am missing a KIDNEY, yes, I'm completely fine," he said, yelling the word kidney, causing Annabelle to jump. Then he laughed. Henrik picked up the coffee cup and slurped loudly as he drank. She wrinkled her nose in disgust.

"I thought about visiting you at the hospital ... but ..."

"Then why didn't you, BITCH?" He said.

"Excuse me?" She said looking perplexed.

"Why didn't you?" He repeated.

"Well they said on TV that you were married. I didn't want to ..."

"Didn't want to what? Didn't want to HARM me? Didn't want to make me SUFFER?"

"I didn't want to destroy your personal life. I mean, I guessed you didn't want your wife to know about me," she said, moving around in her chair like it was uncomfortable to sit in. Henrik discovered he liked to see her squirm in the chair. He liked the way she kept touching her cellphone and holding it close to her in case she needed to call for help. It amused him the way she avoided his eyes. The hand touching her chest and the redness of the skin on her throat. She was nervous. He made her nervous.

"So what can I do for you?" She asked.

"What can I do for you?" He said, imitating her voice, making it sound all shrill and annoying.

She looked at him. She was biting her lip. Then she looked at the phone again and pushed a button like she wanted to make sure it was on. "Listen," she said nervously. Her voice was slightly shivering. "I have to be somewhere ..."

"No you don't," Henrik said.

"Excuse me?"

"You don't have somewhere to be. You're just saying that to get rid of me. Why Annabelle? Why do you want to get rid of me?"

Annabelle blushed. She shook her head and moved her hands fast. "I ... I ..."

"You don't know what to say?" He interrupted her. "Let me help you. I make you feel uncomfortable, don't I?"

She bit her lips and looked at him, then nodded. "Yes. Okay yes. This meeting. You coming here and yelling at me makes me feel slightly uncomfortable."

"Why do you think that is?" Henrik said before slurping more coffee.

"What do you mean?"

"Why do you think me being here makes you feel so uncomfortable?" He asked again, slightly annoyed.

"I don't know ... I guess it might be the yelling, maybe it's just the way you look at me. Like I owe you something. Like you want to ..."

"Like I want to what, Annabelle?"

"Like you want to ... hurt me or something," Annabelle sighed and shook her head. "This conversation is getting a little strange."

"You know what I think is strange?" Henrik asked and didn't wait for her to answer. "I think it's a little strange that I have amazing sex with a woman one night in a hotel and then the next morning ... I wake up and oops, something is missing. Oh my, oh my. Something pretty VITAL is gone from inside of me. Now how on earth did that happen?"

Annabelle covered her mouth. "Oh my God," she exclaimed. "You think ... you think I had something to do with it, don't you?"

"BINGO!" Henrik yelled and slammed his clenched fist into the coffee table causing all the cups to rattle.

Annabelle let out a shriek and got up from her chair. "Get out," she said. "Get out of my apartment right now."

Henrik made the sound of a game show buzzer on TV. "WRONG answer."

"What do you want from me?" She asked with a shivering voice.

Henrik scratched his chin and looked up. "Mmm, let me see. What do I really want from you?"

"I already talked to the police. I told them everything I know. I told them how I met you at the bar. I told them all your bad pick-up lines. I told them about our sex in the hotel room and I told them that I left, that you were awake the last time I saw you and being a real prick."

Henrik laughed manically and slurped more coffee. "Well then, it's all good, isn't it?" He said. "It's absolutely PEACHY." Then his face turned angry. "Except for the fact that I don't buy it."

"It's the truth. I swear. I had nothing to do with what happened to you. Look at me I'm just a little girl. How would I be able to hold you down? I wouldn't even know where to look for the kidney. I faint just seeing blood."

"Ah, come on. Do you really think I'd fall for that? You could have had help, couldn't you? You could have some guy waiting in the hallway once you exited the room and he could have entered the room. It's as simple as that. How much did he pay you, huh?"

"I ... I have no idea what you're talking about. There was no guy. There was only me when I left that night. I might not have closed the door properly, so maybe the guy could have come in that way or something, I don't know. I was pretty pissed at the time. Don't think I worried much about closing the door properly."

Henrik closed his eyes. He was getting sick of this conversation. "How much did he pay you?" He asked again.

"I ... no one paid me anything."

"HOW MUCH?"

"Nothing. Why aren't you listening to what I say? I didn't do anything. I came to the bar to meet a nice guy. Guess that makes me a horrible judge of people, huh?"

"I don't believe you," Henrik said.

"Then what do you want me to say? That I'm sorry? 'Cause I am truly very sorry for what happened to you, but it had nothing to do with me."

"Still don't believe you."

"I'm telling the truth. What do you want from me?"

"I want to know where my kidney is."

"Excuse me?" She asked. "You want what, exactly?"

Henrik got up and stormed towards the girl. He grabbed her around the throat and pushed her backwards against the wall. She was spurting and gasping for air. Henrik kept squeezing while staring into her eyes until no more sound came out of her throat and her body became limp in his hands. Then he let her slide to the ground.

Panting, he bent down and whispered in her ear: "I want to know who has my kidney."

26

SEPTEMBER 2001

ANNA WAS STARING AT the bike, then back at Valdemar. She couldn't believe what she saw. "You made this?" She asked.

The boy nodded. Anna touched the new handlebars that Valdemar had somehow managed to put on the new bike. They were extremely long and bent in a u-shape.

"I made it myself. Using dad's welder."

"You know how I hate it when you use that thing," she said, without being really angry. This was truly spectacular. You couldn't even tell that the handlebars didn't originally belong to the bike.

"But how ... how does it work?" She asked anxiously. It was hard to picture how Valdemar was supposed to use this.

"Take it outside and I'll show you," he said.

"I can put it on the grass so you won't hurt yourself when you fall," Anna said feeling very nervous about the whole thing.

She dragged the bike out of the garage and onto the grass where she put it up against the big birch tree in the front yard. Then she turned and looked at Valdemar with her heart in her throat.

All this for what? To impress his dad? To show him he is good enough? That he is worthy of his love?

Anna felt the tears press from behind her eyes, but held them back. This was a happy moment for Valdemar. He didn't need to see her cry. Valdemar turned and smiled at his mother. She smiled back and gave him a thumbs-up. By putting his head on the handlebars and using his mouth and toes, he climbed onto the bike. Anna jumped forward when he was about to slip down, but stopped herself.

He can do this. You know he can. If he wants it bad enough. You know he can. He has proven it before.

Valdemar managed somehow, someway to get to the seat and sit on it, then he bent forward enough for his shoulders to reach the extremely long handlebars. Anna gasped as he put his feet on the pedals, set off and, very shakily, rode across the lawn.

Oh my God, he's going to kill himself on that thing.

But to her amazement, he didn't. He didn't even fall. Using his head and shoulders to steer, he bicycled down the street, turned around and came back. Anna stood with both her hands covering her mouth. She had stopped breathing and everything inside of her was frozen.

Valdemar rode the thing all the way back on the grass, before he tipped over and landed with the bike op top of him. Anna stormed to him, thinking she could hear him cry, but as she came close, she realized he was, in fact, laughing. The wondrousness of a child's laughter made everything inside of her come alive again and, while helping him get back up, she started laughing too. Laughing with relief and hope thinking that maybe, just maybe it was going to be all right after all. He was going to be alright. Valdemar was not pitiful, he was one of the strongest children this earth was ever going to see.

"Did you see me, Mom? Did you see it?"

"I did, sweetheart. I saw you. I saw everything. It was amazing. You're amazing, Valdemar. You truly are."

Then they laughed again. Finally Anna took the boy inside and brought out ice cream, Valdemar's favorite, and they ate it talking all afternoon about how amazing it felt for him to be able to move around using a bike. How much freedom it gave him.

"It was almost like flying, Mommy."

The next day, he was practicing his biking while Anna watched with anxious eyes and lots of gasps when, all of a sudden, a car drove down the street and into the driveway. Anna's heart dropped.

It was Michael.

He got out of the car and looked at Valdemar as he rode the bike into the driveway and jumped off with a huge smile.

"Did you see it Daddy? Did you see me?" He asked hopefully.

Anna's heart was pounding awaiting the answer. Not a sound left Michael's lips, so Valdemar tried again.

"I'm riding my new bike, Daddy. Just like an ordinary kid I'm riding a bike, a real bike, aren't you proud?"

Come one Michael. Just say something nice for once. Just look at the boy and talk to him. Just this once, you bastard.

But Michael didn't say anything to Valdemar. Instead he turned his head and faced Anna with the words:

"I'm leaving you."

27

AUGUST 2012

WE CHECKED IN TO Hotel Mercury in Silkeborg around five thirty in the afternoon. We agreed to meet for dinner in the restaurant at six thirty after taking a rest. I sat on the bed with my cellphone in my hand finding the courage to call Peter and let him know what was going on. I had wanted to wait till I was alone, since I didn't want Sune to know if Peter got upset. It was Julie who picked up the phone. My heart was beating. Hearing her voice made me miss her like crazy.

"Hi sweetie. How is everything?"

"Great," she said.

"What are you doing?"

"Playing Mindskill on the iPad."

I smiled. That was all she did lately. Playing Mindskill or watching videos on YouTube of other people playing it. I didn't get it. To me it was just a world of big blocks and it seemed really boring, but all the kids loved it. "Of course you are. What is your father doing?"

"Taking a shower. He's been painting all day. He said he was going to make pancakes for dinner."

"Oh, did he now?"

"Yeah. He also said you couldn't do anything about it since you weren't here."

I laughed. "Well he is right. I guess it will do for tonight. Your dad makes wonderful pancakes. That's the one thing he can actually make."

"I know. So when are you coming back? Dad said, since you weren't here yet, you probably wouldn't make it for dinner."

"He's right. I have to stay the night. Will you be alright alone?" I asked.

"I'm not alone. Dad's here, remember?" She said.

"Of course. Just making sure you don't miss me too much."

"You have high thoughts about yourself, Mommy. Of course I miss you, but I'll see you tomorrow right?"

"Yes, baby. I'm doing a late interview here tonight, then I'll sleep and go right back to Brabrand tomorrow morning."

"Is Sune with you?" She asked.

I paused. "Yes. Yes he is. We're working together."

"What about Tobias?"

"He's at home with a nanny," I answered. "Sune will go home to be with him tomorrow morning."

"Oh okay." Her voice sounded disappointed. I wondered if she had thought I would bring Sune and Tobias with me back to the island. "Here is daddy."

"Hi there." Peter sounded happy.

"Hi. Listen. They want me to stay the night. I have an interview late tonight. I'll be back tomorrow instead."

Peter went quiet. A million thoughts ran through my mind while trying to figure out what he was thinking and feeling. "Okay," he said. "I had a feeling that it was going to be late since we hadn't heard from you and you hadn't come back yet. But I hadn't expected you to stay away all night. I guess I'll have to live with it, then."

"It's just that they have landed an interview with the kidney-guy and he is only going to be around for tonight. Tomorrow he is going back to Roskilde."

"Well you do what you gotta do. We'll be here waiting for you." Peter sighed and paused. "Say, is Sune staying at the hotel with you?"

I closed my eyes. "Yes." I exhaled and rubbed my forehead. "He is staying in another room."

"Well I sure hope he is," Peter said. "Why wouldn't he be?"

"No. That's not what I meant ..."

"No, I know what you meant. You think I'm jealous, don't you?" Peter sounded offended, all of a sudden.

"Well ... I guess."

"Do I have any reason to be jealous?" He asked.

I froze. I wanted so badly to tell him he didn't, but I knew it would be a lie. Seeing Sune again had awoken a lot of emotions in me that I didn't want him to know about. Feelings that I hardly wanted to admit to myself that I had.

"No. No. Of course not. I'll see you tomorrow."

"See you then."

28

AUGUST 2012

"SO HOW ARE JULIE and your dad?"

Sune looked at me after we had ordered and the waiter had left. I felt like I was already cheating on Peter just by sitting in the hotel restaurant with Sune.

I smiled. "They're both fine. Well that's not completely true. Julie is great. My dad's health is still not too good. He's had a lot of infections and problems with his bladder lately. I keep hoping it'll get better, and some days he's doing really great, but then a new infection comes along that he has trouble beating and we're back to where we started. He had a bladder infection just last week that ..." I paused and looked up at Sune. "I'm sharing a little too much here. You don't want to hear those details."

Sune raised his hand to stop me. "No, I do. I love your dad, you know that. I don't mind hearing details."

"Okay. Well it's not something we should talk about at the dinner table, but he is fighting, and hopefully winning, but it is getting harder for him to do simple things, like walking on his own, getting out of the house and so on. I have my sister looking out for him while we're gone, but I don't know if ... I mean, she has small kids and a fulltime job and all ..."

"I can check in on him when I get back to Karrebaeks-minde if you'd like."

I look at him and our eyes locked. "Would you do that? It would be a great help for me. I am so concerned constantly."

Sune smiled. The waiter brought our food. "Of course, Rebekka. I'd do anything for you."

I sipped my wine, feeling my heart racing. I had no idea what to say to that, so I started eating instead. The duck was terrible. I took one bite, then looked at Sune who had picked the same as me. I chewed and chewed, but it was so hard to chew I wondered if I would ever be able to swallow it. Sune looked like he had the same troubles. Then I laughed. Sune chuckled and finally swallowed. I did the same, before we both flushed it down with the red wine.

"How can anyone ruin duck?" I whispered and leaned over the table.

Sune laughed. "I don't know. You'd have to be pretty good, I guess."

I chuckled and pushed the meat aside, then tried the potatoes. They weren't as bad as the meat, but they weren't good either.

"Wow. I never thought I would ever taste anything worse than the food I had in juvenile prison," Sune said.

I burst into laughter. I looked at his hand missing the two fingers that he had lost in prison when he was doing time for hacking as a teenager. I had heard all his stories from the inside and knew all about how tough it had been on him. In a very few years, I had gotten to know him better than I knew my own husband, who never told me anything from his past. I had to always drag it out of him. Sune wasn't like that. Sune could talk about his emotions, about stuff he had gone through. Peter couldn't. Peter had grown up in an environment where you weren't allowed to discuss your feelings. Where it was considered as a weakness. That much he had told me, but that was about it. I never met his parents since they lived in Singapore now, where his father had his business. I had met his brother on one occasion, but only briefly when he was in Aarhus many years ago. I felt like Peter didn't want me to know his family and, in the beginning of my marriage, it annoyed me and made me feel like he was embarrassed by me, but after some time, I realized that it had nothing to do with me. It wasn't me he was embarrassed by; it was his family.

Sune had become silent. He was looking at me with serious eyes. I sensed he was going to say something. My heart was beating fast and I felt my cheeks blush. I thought like crazy about something to say to break the silence.

"So how is Tobias?" I asked.

"Good. He misses Julie, though."

I nodded and drank. "I know. Julie misses him too. She was just asking for him on the phone when I was in my room. She thought he was with you here."

"That's sweet."

Sune exhaled. "Rebekka ... I ..." He grabbed my hand.

I shook my head and pulled my hand away. "Don't Sune. Don't do this."

Sune pulled back and bit his lip. "Okay. I get it. I'm gonna leave it there. This is the way you want it. I get it."

A new silence broke out between us. A waiter approached us. He looked at me. "Mrs. Franck?"

"Yes?"

"Mr. Fenger is waiting for you in the bar."

I looked at my watch. "He's early," I said.

29

AUGUST 2012

SHE WAS PRETTIER THAN he thought she would be. Henrik Fenger didn't exactly know what he had expected, but not this. He watched her from afar, in the mirror behind the bartender, as she walked out from the restaurant and towards him in the bar. Her searching eyes scanning the area to find him gave her away. Behind her followed a younger guy, very tall and who looked more like a punker than a photographer.

"Mr. Fenger?"

Henrik grinned and turned on his bar stool. "Rebekka Franck I assume?" He reached out his hand and she took it. Nice firm handshake. He liked that in a woman. Probably a feisty little one.

"This is my photographer Sune Johansen," she said introducing the punk-guy behind her.

"Hi," he said and reached out his hand.

"Hello," Henrik said and shook his hand slightly, reluctantly wondering what kind of germs and following diseases this guy was going to give him. Henrik stared at the photographer's ring in the eyebrow. He wrinkled his nose. He never understood why people wanted rings all over the place that could get infected.

"Let's go sit in the corner over there," Rebekka Franck said and pointed at some couches.

"Can I get you anything to drink?" Henrik asked. He couldn't stop staring at the woman. She was beautiful, not in a traditional way, but there was just something about her, something alluring that made him want to screw her.

"No, we just ate," Rebekka said.

"Ah come on," Henrik said. "You look like someone who would enjoy a Chardonnay."

"As a matter of fact, I'm more of a red wine person," she said.

"Then let me buy you a glass of red wine," Henrik insisted. Before she could protest, he ordered one for her.

"I'll just have a beer," the photographer said.

He was already annoying Henrik and he was starting to wonder how he was going to get rid of him. Henrik moaned slightly in pain as he got up from his bar stool and walked towards the black leather couches in the corner.

"Do you need a hand?" Rebekka Franck asked.

"No." Henrik said a little too harshly. "I mean, I'm fine. Just the damn pain that won't go away."

"From the surgery?" Sune the photographer asked.

No from fucking all night. Yes of course it's from having my kidney removed you idiot!

"It must have been quite painful?" Rebekka Franck asked.

Henrik loathed the tone of pity in her voice. Yes, he was the victim, but no he didn't want to be treated like a cripple. He wanted her to see how handsome he was, how attractive he was. Henrik always had a way with the ladies.

"It wasn't so bad," he said, trying hard to smile.

"Oh my God," Rebekka Franck suddenly said and pointed at his white shirt.

"What?"

"I think you're bleeding," she said. "Is that blood on your shirt? There on the right side?"

Henrik looked down. Her had taken a shower after killing Annabelle and put on new clothes so he hardly thought it could be hers, but suddenly he feared it was. "It's nothing," he said, and smiled.

"Don't you think we should take you to the hospital?" Sune the photographer asked.

He shook his head while imagining himself smashing the boy's face in with a clenched fist. "No it's nothing. I can hardly feel anything. The doctor said this might happen."

They sat down on the couches and Henrik found a handkerchief in his pocket that he wiped his forehead with. He was sweating heavily now.

"You don't look too well," Rebekka Franck said. "Maybe we should do this another day?"

"No," Henrik said, annoyed with all the fussing. Yes, the doctor had told him to rest and stay calm, but how could he? How could he remain at peace with so many IDIOTS in this world?

Henrik wiped his forehead again, then forced a smile and looked at Rebekka Franck. "Shall we begin?"

30

AUGUST 2012

BILL DURGIN WAS SITTING in the bar with an iPad on the counter. The bartender had served up a beer while Bill was looking for the next lucky victim. Meanwhile, Bill was in the chat room, talking to one of the other artists.

I'm sitting in the bar at the hotel now.

Oh, the thrill of the chase, someone named Karl Persson answered. Bill had been chatting with him before. He was quite the lunatic, but very good at inspiring and giving good advice.

Spotted your next victim yet? He asked.

I have my eyes on several right now. Bill was looking up into the mirror behind the bartender, where observing the guests in the hotel without being seen was a lot easier. A guy at the end of the bar looked promising.

Ah I love this part, Karl wrote. *Scanning the room, knowing you hold the power of life and death in your hand, knowing you get to choose who will live to see tomorrow and who won't.*

Bill had to admit, it was enjoyable. Who could have ever guessed, but Thomas De Quincey had been right. After the first kill, the thought of the next one was much easier; it was almost thrilling. It provided the ultimate satisfaction to hurt these people. These people who deserved nothing better, who had it coming to them.

Cheating bastards.

A woman sat in the corner with a tall punk fellow and another man who had his back to Bill. They were talking; the punk fellow was taking pictures of the guy who had his back turned. Bill studied the woman and the punker. They didn't look like a couple. He was way younger than her. But they had dinner at the restaurant earlier in the night and seemed very comfortable, stealing looks and looking at each other like they weren't supposed to be together, like they were afraid to be caught. Bill could smell an affair from far away and those two had one. The tension in the air between them was electrifying. There was no doubt. They smelled of deceit.

I have my eye on two right now. I might do them both this time.

You go for it. A double kill is very rare. Did one back in '89. I can still remember the thrill. I live to relive it.

Bill chuckled and drank the beer. A man entered the bar and sat two stools down from Bill. He smiled and nodded. Bill smiled back.

"How's the beer?" The man asked.

"To die for," Bill answered.

The man laughed awkwardly. Bill turned to look at the couple again. The punker was laughing, looking at the woman who apparently had said something funny. A chill ran down Bill's spine. It was disgusting. The way they looked at each other was repulsive.

What about your husband at home, little lady? The young boy didn't look like he was married with children, but the woman probably was. She looked like it. It was in her eyes, her entire body was smeared in it. The way she looked at the boy when she talked and then looked down quickly afterwards made her look guilty. Tormented by it.

So have you chosen? Karl asked.

I think I have.

When will you strike?

At midnight when they're all asleep. They'll never know what hit them. It'll be a night of terror. A punishment to fit the crime.

You're evil.

The woman laughed again. The hair rose on the back of Bill's neck. The falseness, the dishonesty to her voice was creepy. A woman like her deserved to die.

31

AUGUST 2012

I LAUGHED AWKWARDLY AT my own joke. The whole situation was a little strange and felt clumsy. Sune and I tried hard to lighten the atmosphere a little, but with no luck. Henrik Fenger was a strange man who seemed to be in way too much pain to be sitting here when he should be in a hospital. He was sweating heavily and he seemed to be bleeding too. I didn't quite know what to say to him, but I really thought he should go to the hospital.

As we spoke and he told his story, he kept groaning and moaning in pain. Then he found some pills in his jacket and swallowed a couple, flushing them down with beer. I asked him several times if we should drive him to the nearest hospital, but he refused. It felt highly uncomfortable for both me and Sune, but the man had, after all, the right to decide not to go. It was a very strange situation and an even weirder interview. The man seemed so uncomfortable and, every now and then, he would yell at me and hit his fist on the table holding our drinks. I started wondering if he was really well. Not just physically. He seemed to have a huge amount of anger trapped inside of him. It made him a little scary.

"So how did you feel when you heard about the second case in Hasle?" I asked.

Henrik Fenger froze in the middle of drinking. He put the glass down very hard on the table. "The what?" He asked.

I looked at Sune, then back at Henrik Fenger. "You didn't hear about the man who was killed at a hotel in Hasle?"

Henrik Fenger looked confused. "What?"

"It was very similar to your story, except he didn't survive," I continued. "His liver was removed and he died overnight. The cleaning lady found him covered in ice just like you were."

"But ..." Henrik Fenger stared at me like there was something really wrong with me. "You say he died?"

I nodded and drank from my wine. I looked up at the bar. It was strange. I kept having the feeling that someone was watching me. Maybe it was just the entire situation that made me a little paranoid. It was stupid, really, but the thought of having to spend the night in a hotel scared me a little. I couldn't help thinking: *what if I wake up covered in ice? What if they take one of my organs?*

I shook my head. No it was ridiculous. There were so many hotels. To have the organ thieves strike right at the one I was staying in was hardly realistic. Or was it? I felt a chill and looked up at the bar behind Henrik Fenger again. Was someone observing me?

I looked at Henrik Fenger again. He seemed to be getting worse. He was sweating heavily and panting. He was still staring at me. I tried to smile.

"Anyway, that's all I know," I said.

"What do the police say?" Henrik Fenger asked. His voice was shrill.

"Apparently, he was with some girl on the night it happened. They have her in custody now."

Henrik Fenger looked like he was choking. He put his beer down. "She's WHAT?" He said yelling the last word with a shrill voice.

"She's been taken into police custody to be interrogated. But I spoke to one of the officers when I was in my room earlier and he told me they will be letting her go in the morning. She doesn't know anything, he told me."

Henrik Fenger's right eye started blinking and he was moving his head in a weird way reminding me of the pigeons I used to feed with Julie in the center of Copenhagen when she was younger.

"Are you sure you're okay?" Sune asked.

Henrik Fenger grinned. "Yes. Yes. I'm okay. Why shouldn't I be? Huh? Tell me WHY? Because someone stole my kidney? Because my wife won't answer my calls? Huh? Is that it? Because I'm sitting here with two MORONS who don't understand ANTYHING? Because the whole damn world has gone MAD overnight?"

I turned to face Sune and our eyes met. He made a grimace. I fought hard not to laugh. I got up and reached out my hand.

"I think we have what we came for. Thank you so much, Mr. Fenger for taking time to meet with us."

I shook his hand and Henrik Fenger grumbled something as Sune and I hurried to get away from him. As we left the bar, I couldn't let go of the feeling that someone was still watching my every move, so I turned and looked. I met a set of eyes in the mirror behind the bartender. They seemed friendly, so I smiled. The eyes smiled back.

32

SEPTEMBER 2001

"COULD YOU AT LEAST tell me why?"

Anna's voice was shivering as she spoke. Michael was packing a suitcase, throwing shirts and pants randomly into it. He hadn't spoken a word since he had told her he was leaving and Anna felt both frustrated and confused. She wanted to grab on to him and shake him. But she had felt that for a long time. She simply didn't understand how he could be so cruel ... the same man she had loved and wanted to spend her life with.

"Please, Michael. Don't do this to us," she pleaded desperately. She kept wondering what she could say or do to make him stay.

But Michael didn't even look at her as he packed his stuff. It was like he couldn't get out of the house fast enough, like he couldn't get out of their lives fast enough.

"Michael you have a son, for Christ sake!" She yelled, when he closed the suitcase and lifted it up. "You have a responsibility. You made a vow to me once. You have a family."

Finally Michael looked at her. Anna's heart was beating

so fast now. She wanted to punch him, hug him, and hold on to him all at the same time. She didn't do any of those things. Instead, she just stared at him with a feeling of utter desperation exploding inside of her.

"He was never my son, you know that," Michael said. "He was a mistake from the beginning."

Anna clenched her fist and smashed it as hard as she could into his face. Michael let out a scream and flew backwards. Michael's nose was bleeding when he looked at her again. He wiped the blood off with his hand.

"I have a new family now," he said. "A real one."

"What the hell is that supposed to mean? How can you have a new family?" Anna asked, confused.

Michael looked into her eyes. "If you must know, I've had another family for a number of years now. I am with them when I'm not here."

Anna's heart dropped. She had to hold on to the frame of the door to not fall. She couldn't believe what he was telling her. It was like a bad dream, a nightmare that wouldn't end.

"What do you mean you have another family? I don't understand? How?"

"Well, it's been going fine until last week when she found out about you and Valdemar. She asked me to choose between the two of you. And I chose her. Her and ... Patrick."

Anna stumbled backwards. Patrick? Not only did he have another woman but also another son? "Patrick?" She said with a shaking voice. "Is that ...?"

Michael looked at her with such coldness and cruelty she could no longer understand how she could have loved him.

"He is my son," Michael said.

Anna heard something and turned her head to see Valdemar standing right next to them. His eyes were filled with tears. Anna realized he must have heard the entire discussion between her and Michael.

"Mommy?" He said. "Who ... Who is Patrick?"

For the first time since Valdemar was born, Michael looked directly into his eyes and spoke:

"He's my real son."

Then he lifted up the suitcase and stormed past the boy. Anna's entire body was shaking when she ran to grab Valdemar in her arms. She lifted him up and held him close to her body. For days after this, Valdemar never spoke a word. He didn't ride his bike nor did he go into the garage for a long, long time.

33

AUGUST 2012

SUNE AND I COULDN'T stop laughing. We had gone back to Sune's hotel room, room 237 and were going through the interview and pictures together.

"Can you believe that guy?" Sune asked.

"I don't think I can," I said, chuckling.

We grabbed a couple of beers from the minibar while we worked. "Look at this one," Sune said and showed me a picture he had taken of Henrik Fenger while he spoke. "The guy looks like he is about to explode."

"Did you see the tic, he had?" I said.

"And what was with the yelling of certain words?" Sune said.

"It's actually not funny," I said, still laughing.

"I know. It's really sad. The guy seemed to have some serious anger management issues."

"I tried not to laugh, but it was hard. There was just something about the guy that was so comical, I couldn't help it. I have always felt that way with angry people. I never could take them seriously. I hope I wasn't inappropriate," I said and opened my laptop.

"You were fine. He liked you. It was me he couldn't stand," Sune said. "He kept staring at the ring in my eyebrow like he wanted to rip it out. I think I was the one provoking him. My appearance does that to people from time to time. If I had a penny for every time an old lady tried to beat me with her cane because she thought I was going to rob her or something ... well I'd have a lot of pennies."

"You do look pretty provoking," I said with a grin. I opened a Word document and started typing my article. I felt Sune's eyes on me. I didn't turn to look at him. The air between us had been strange and almost tense all night. I fought the urge to kiss him like nothing I had ever fought in my life.

"Well, you always look great," Sune said. "I think the guy wanted to be alone with you. That's why he resented me so much. He wanted me out of the way so he could make a pass at you."

I laughed. "You've got to be kidding me. The man was in so much pain. He is sick. And I don't just mean physically. There was something really wrong with him. He was kind of creepy, really."

Sune uploaded his pictures while I wrote my article, trying hard to be as nice to the guy as possible and present him like a sane person. When I was done, I sent it to my editor and looked at Sune. He was looking at me too. I didn't like the look in his eyes and looked away.

"So I guess that's it, huh?" I said and closed the lid of my laptop.

Sune picked up his camera and was looking at me through the lens. I could tell he was zooming in on me. Then he took a series of pictures.

"Stop it," I said. "I look terrible."

"I don't think so," Sune said, then took a series more. He got up from his chair and started moving around while taking more pictures of me.

"Sune. You know I don't like to be photographed."

I lied. The fact was, I really liked it when he took pictures of me. I liked when he was watching me, looking at me through the lens of the camera, studying me. My heart was beating faster as he came closer. He lowered the camera and looked me into my eyes. Then he leaned over and kissed me.

The kiss felt incredible. Like an explosion on my lips. It didn't feel like I was cheating on Peter. It felt so right and that made it so difficult.

"Stay with me tonight," Sune whispered once our lips parted.

I exhaled, then kissed him again. I fought the urge, but in vain. I kissed him again and again, then held him in my arms and felt like crying. It was like my body had missed this, missed being close to his. It was like I was depriving my body of something vital when I wasn't with him.

But when you're not with Peter, you're depriving your daughter of a father, of having a real family, aren't you?

I pushed Sune away and got up. I grabbed my laptop and threw it in my bag. "Rebekka," Sune pleaded. He grabbed my hand. Our eyes locked.

"Stay. Please stay here."

I stroked his cheek gently. My entire body was screaming madly at me as I made up my mind. "I'm sorry," I said. "I'm going back tonight."

34

AUGUST 2012

BILL DURGIN FOLLOWED THE chosen couple through the hallway of the hotel and watched as they went into a room together.

I knew it! Nothing but cheating bastards. Going in there to fuck are we? Going to spend the night together making passionate love and then go home to your families the next day and pretend like nothing ever happened, are we?

Bill Durgin growled, put down the equipment-filled briefcase, pulled out the dry erase marker and held it for a little while thinking about its origin and felt such a deep sadness.

The marker was used to open the lock on the door to the room next to them. Luckily, it was empty. Bill sat down and pulled out the iPad, hoping that Thomas De Quincey would be in the chat room, but he wasn't. Instead, to Karl Persson:

Picked my target. Now all I have to do is wait.
Good for you. Will you post pictures?
Sure.

Good. I will be waiting for them. Got myself a little treat today as well, Karl Persson wrote.

I thought you were laying low? Someone called Michael Cogliantry answered. He had just joined the chat.

I was. But I couldn't resist. It was like taking candy from a kid. There was no way I was just going to let a chance like this pass me by, Karl wrote.

Who was she? Michael Cogliantry asked.

A girl around sixteen who walks past in the street every day on her way home from school. I have watched her for weeks, followed her everywhere. This afternoon I followed her from afar as she walked home. For the first time, she was alone. No one was walking with her and not a soul was in sight, even if it was broad daylight. As she put the key in the lock to her apartment building, I walked up behind her and grabbed her. I raped her in the basement of her own damn building with her parents probably drinking tea and waiting for her to come home just upstairs. Then I stabbed her, found a saw, cut her into pieces, and threw the remains in the dumpster behind the building. They'll empty it early in the morning. No one will ever know where she has gone. I slipped out and walked home without anyone seeing me. It was perfect. So delightful. I feel refreshed. Born again.

Sounds a little risky if you ask me, Cogliantry wrote. *You know it is dangerous to kill too close to home. And in broad daylight? Are you crazy? Remember what happened to Einaudi.*

Einaudi was crazy. He ran amok. I'm not him and never will be, Karl Persson argued.

How do you know? To me, it sounds like you're taking way too many risks. I don't want to be exposed just because you're not being careful.

Why are you fighting? It was Thomas De Quincey. He

had joined the chat. Bill Durgin smiled in the hotel room and listened to the couple talking loudly on the other side of the wall. Finally, Thomas was on.

This isn't a chat room for people fighting, he continued. *This is all about supporting one another, remember? It's about sharing experiences and helping each other out. Artists like us can be very lonely, especially with our kind of art. This is the only place we can share our masterpieces. I will not have people fighting in here ... or you're out.*

You're right, Cogliantry wrote.

Sorry for that, Karl Persson wrote.

It always amazed Bill how much authority and power Thomas De Quincey held over the others in the chat room. Bill was new to the whole thing and was quite fascinated with this Thomas character. You could say he had been a mentor.

This is Bill's night, Thomas De Quincey wrote. *It's his time to shine. He is coming more and more together as an artist and we should encourage and support him for that. How's your next work coming along?*

Bill smiled and heard the voices become even louder in the room next door. *Very good. Doing a couple this time.*

Very good, Thomas De Quincey answered. *A double murder. You're progressing.*

Well I have to, don't I? Progress towards the Grand Finale, Bill wrote.

And then your masterpiece is ready. I love what you are doing here. That the world will never understand nor appreciate your work only makes you an even greater artist, Bill.

Bill smiled again. There was no one who could encourage like Thomas De Quincey. The voices had stopped next door and Bill wondered if they were having sex. Waiting until they were done, Bill looked back at the iPad when suddenly, a door shut. Was that? Could it be?

Bill stood up, put the iPad away, and rushed into the hallway just in time to see the woman storm down the hallway and into an elevator. This was way too early. Bill cursed and stomped, then fondled the marker as though it was a talisman. Looking at the door, Bill wondered if leaving now might be the best idea.

No, that would be a shame. There was still one person in there guilty of adultery.

35

AUGUST 2012

I CALLED PETER FROM the car on my way back and told him I was coming back. He was so happy, he told me and he was going to stay awake to wait for me. I kissed him when he opened the door and threw myself in his arms.

"I'm so sorry," I said. "I'm so sorry for everything."

Peter chuckled and stroked my cheek. "It's okay, Rebekka. I'm beginning to get how important your job is to you."

I smiled and kissed him again, wondering for one insane second if he could taste Sune on my lips. Could he taste that I had kissed someone else?

We went inside and up to bed where Peter wanted to have sex, but I told him I was way too tired. He looked disappointedly at me.

"Tomorrow, Peter. Today I'm beat after a long day. I just want to go to sleep."

Peter kissed my nose and turned around to go to sleep. I lay a long time with my eyes open, staring into the old, hand-carved, wooden ceiling, and feeling like the worst person on earth. I had been lying to Peter. I wasn't too beat to have sex. The fact was I didn't want to. I hadn't felt attracted to him.

Probably just because you're so damn confused.

I closed my eyes and forced myself to think about something else and finally, after half an hour or so, I fell into a heavy sleep.

"Mommy! Mommy! You're back." Julie woke me up the next morning jumping into our bed with a shriek. I grabbed her and hugged her for a long time. "What do you want to do today?" she asked.

"I want to do anything you want," I said and looked into her eyes.

"Let's play hide and seek," she said.

"Okay. After breakfast."

"Do you want to play too, Daddy?" Julie said.

"I guess I could play a little," he answered.

"How's the painting going?" I asked. I looked at my family and felt suddenly overwhelmed with gratefulness. To think I had almost thrown all of that away again.

"Not progressing as fast as I'd like it to," Peter said. "But, alright I guess."

"Let's go," Julie yelled and jumped down from the bed.

"I'll take a shower first," I said. "Be right down."

I walked into the bathroom, when suddenly I felt incredibly nauseated. It was overpowering and I had to sit down on the bathroom floor.

It's gotta be stress, I thought to myself.

I undressed and looked at myself in the mirror. Had my breasts grown? They had been very sore lately and now I could hardly touch them. Another wave of nausea flushed over me and I barely made it to the toilet before I threw up.

It was when I lifted my head and spotted the box of Tampax on the shelf that the penny finally dropped.

Could it be? Could I be? No. No. No.

I went through the stuff in my toilet bag, knowing I had hidden a pregnancy test somewhere in it from back when I was with Sune. I had used one of these a month, only to disappoint him with the results.

With a beating heart, I pulled out the stick and peed on it. Then I waited, but I didn't even have to wait till the time was up before I had my answer. I couldn't believe my eyes. I checked the box again, hoping I was wrong, hoping I had misunderstood it. Nope. I hadn't. *Two lines shows you're pregnant* it said.

I had to sit down. I stormed into the bedroom and sat on the bed staring at the small stick with the very serious message, wondering whom the father could be.

Was it Peter? If so, then there was no problem. We were a family and now, an expanding one. Nothing wrong with that.

Except the fact that you'd have to say a definitive goodbye to Sune. The thought hurt me deeply.

But could the child be Sune's? We had tried for months without any luck. Maybe it had finally paid off? In that case, I would end up hurting both Peter and Julie. I would crush the dream of a family. Sune would be thrilled beyond anything, since he had wanted another child for all the time I had known him. But what about me? I looked at the stick again, then down at my stomach that suddenly seemed to have grown tremendously in the last five minutes.

Did I really want another child? Did I want to destroy my family to have it?

36

AUGUST 2012

HENRIK FENGER WAS TRYING to run, but it hurt too much. He stopped for a little while to catch his breath, leaning towards the wall of a building. The bleeding had stopped and he had felt better waking up in his hotel room this morning. Last night had been a disaster for him. He had felt so confused and angry after talking to that journalist woman and after learning that there had been another victim like him. At first, he had freaked out thinking he had killed the wrong girl, but after a good night's sleep, he finally saw things clearly now.

They were in on it together. The both of them had worked together on this. Two whores picking up guys in bars just to sedate them and steal their organs at night. It was very simple really. That was the only explanation he could come up with. Maybe there were even more than two? Maybe they were an entire group of women working this way. Maybe getting their revenge over men, who hadn't been treating them right or something.

That was it. A group of man-hating, freaking feminists. Maybe they were even trying to prove a point or something.

Maybe they were like activists trying to tell people something through their desperate and violent actions.

Freaking feminists. Thinking they can have it all, thinking that they are as good as men. Bah.

Henrik looked at the piece of paper with the address in his hand, then at the iPhone where he had plotted the address in the app called maps. He had parked the rented car far away, so it wouldn't be seen. He had to turn right at the next corner and then left on the first street. Henrik looked up the hill thinking it was going to be hard for him to walk all that way. Then he thought of Annabelle and how she had been deceiving him all night, whispering sweet words in his ear telling him how handsome he was, how she enjoyed being with him. Henrik growled and felt the adrenalin rush through his veins. Anger was the best drive he could think of. He roared and started walking again, now with renewed strength while picturing this Barbara character doing all the same things to this guy who she had ended up killing.

"Barbara Rasmussen," he mumbled.

He had gotten the name from the bartender at the hotel in Hasle where the other guy had been killed. Martin Damsgaard was his name. It was a name Henrik was going to make sure Barbara Rasmussen wasn't going to forget anytime soon. Martin wasn't here to take his own revenge, so Henrik would do it for him. It was the least he could do. Make sure these women realized they weren't getting away with this, even if the police were too stupid to see what was going on.

Henrik had paid the bartender five hundred kroner to give him the name and address of the girl. The bartender told him he had slept with her once, himself, at her place, so he knew exactly where to find her.

Henrik turned a corner and walked some hundred yards until he finally found the street where Barbara lived. It didn't take him long to spot the right building. A garbage truck further up the street emptied the dumpsters. A couple of neighbors were talking in a door opening.

"You hear about Jessen's daughter in number fourteen?"

"Yes terrible story. You think she ran away from home?"

"Nils in number twelve B says he saw her walk home yesterday afternoon after school, as usual. She passed his window at three o'clock, but she never made it home, her parents say."

"You think they're lying? They have beaten her before, remember?"

"Ah yes, terrible story."

Henrik shook his head and walked past the chatting women, not caring that they saw his face. Women weren't his favorite species among humans right now. He fought an urge to yell at them, to scare them senseless and give them something real to talk about. But this was not why he had come here.

37

AUGUST 2012

I WAS CLOSE TO tears as I walked down the stairs to eat breakfast. I had been thinking about it over and over again, but had not come up with any good solutions to my situation. So, I decided to try and ignore it. At least for a couple of hours while playing with my daughter, spending time with my family. Whatever happened, I didn't want to ruin this vacation for Julie. My editor had been calling my phone and leaving messages, but I hadn't listened to them or called him back, since I wasn't in the mood to work today. Today he would have to find someone else.

When I walked inside the kitchen, the TV was on and both Julie and Peter were staring at it.

"What's going on?" I asked.

"Looks like you have to work again, Mommy," Julie said.

"What do you mean?"

"It happened again," Peter said. "Someone was attacked at a hotel in Silkeborg."

My heart stopped. "In Silkeborg. I was just there yesterday. What hotel? What hotel, Peter?"

"Easy now, Rebekka. I don't know the name of the hotel."

"Hotel Mercury," Julie said. I stared at her. My heart stopped.

"Who was the victim? Have they told who it was yet?" I asked.

"No. They don't know yet. All they know is that some guy was attacked in his hotel room and was found covered in ice cubes in the bathtub. They say he had his spleen taken out."

"Oh my God. Is he alive?"

"He was airlifted to the hospital in Aarhus. That's all they've said, so far."

I felt nauseated and had to sit down to not faint. "Are you okay, Mommy?" Julie asked. I felt her hand on my neck. It was like the room was spinning around me and I was suffocating at the same time. I wasn't sure I could stand up. The pregnancy, the decisions, the prospect of having to let them all down, and now this?

I reached into my pocket and found my phone. I found Sune's number and called it. Peter looked at me while I waited for an answer. But none came. His voicemail started and I hung up.

Peter was still looking at me. "What's going on, Rebekka?"

I shook my head and tried to call Sune again. Still no answer. This time I left a message on his voicemail.

"It's Rebekka. Call me when you get this."

I hung up. Peter had an angry look to his eyes. "It's him, isn't it? You're worried about that Sune guy, right?"

"What?" Julie said. "What about Sune?"

My hands were sweaty. I wiped them on my pants. My heart was racing like crazy. I felt like crying. Why the hell wasn't he answering his phone? Sune always answered his phone. This couldn't be ... it simply couldn't be happening. A thousand thoughts ran through my mind and I had no time to consider Peter's jealousy or emotions at this point.

"Rebekka, I think you're exaggerating here. You don't know why he isn't answering his phone. Maybe he is still sleeping. Maybe he is already on his way home. He was going by train, right? Maybe he caught an early one?"

I nodded, while pressing back my tears. I had a horrifying feeling inside that something was wrong. I couldn't explain it. I only knew I was certain that something bad had happened to him and I couldn't bear it.

I looked up at Peter. "I need to borrow your car again," I said. "I have to go back to the hotel."

I got up from the chair and started packing my bag again. Peter exhaled. "Rebekka is this really necessary?"

"I'm afraid so, Peter. I have to do this. I have to make sure he is alright. Besides Jens-Ole probably wants me to cover the story for the paper anyway. He has already called me several times this morning and left messages in my voice-mail. I just haven't called him back yet."

Peter handed me the keys to his Land Rover with a sigh.

"I'm sorry, Peter. But this is something I have to do."

"I don't understand it," Peter said. I detected anger in his voice. "It's not just about the work, is it? It's about him. Is he really that important to you? I'm sure if you wait half an hour he will call you back. Why Rebekka? Why is he still this important to you?"

I kissed Julie and put on my jacket. "I don't know Peter. He just is, alright?"

"Do you still love him?"

"Let's talk about it when I get back. First of all I need to know if he is alright. Then, I think we need to sit down and talk."

Peter growled, then grabbed my arm. It hurt. He pulled me back. "No."

"No what?"

"No you're not going anywhere. You're staying here with me, with us."

I looked into his eyes and suddenly saw the Peter I remembered from back when he wasn't well. I gasped and pulled my arm away.

"Don't ever tell me what to do, Peter. Not ever again."

38

AUGUST 2012

I WAS BOTH FRUSTRATED and angry as I drove across the countryside towards Silkeborg. I kept calling Sune, but he still didn't pick up. I had no idea what to think. On the radio, they talked about the third case of organ theft in the area and interviewed a police officer about how people should approach this, asking him if they should be scared.

"No I don't think that they should. So far, the victims have all been white males and all have been staying in hotels. There is no reason that normal people should be afraid in their homes."

"But maybe if they're staying the night at a hotel?" The journalist asked.

The policeman sighed. "I don't want to spread panic or ruin the hotel business so, no, you're not going to get me to say it is dangerous to stay in a hotel."

I turned the volume down when there was a commercial break and drove on. It was raining now and the winds had picked up a lot. When the commercials were done on the radio, the presenter talked about a storm that was on its way. I tried calling Sune again, but still no answer. I called

Jens-Ole instead and told him I had received his messages and was on my way to the hotel in Silkeborg. Then I asked him if he had heard anything from Sune.

"Not since last night when he sent me the pictures for today's story. Great article by the way."

"Thanks."

"I thought you were with him. Didn't you stay at the same hotel?" He asked.

"No. I went home to be with my family."

"Too bad. I thought I had you on the inside. That would have been a great story," he said.

Yeah, then we could both have been victims and made the front cover, I thought, sarcastically.

"You're not thinking something might have happened to him?" Jens-Ole asked.

"I don't know what I'm thinking. All I know is, he spent the night there at the same hotel and there weren't that many other guests. Is there any news about the identity of the victim?"

"Not yet. My guess is they are looking to inform the relatives first," Jens-Ole said. "I'm sure he is fine, Rebekka."

"I really hope so."

"Call me when you find him." I detected a slight concern in Jens-Ole's voice.

"I will."

I hung up and continued through the many hills and forests thinking of nothing else but Sune and all the fun times we had had together. I thought about Tobias back at home in Karrebaeksminde. Who was going to tell him?

You're being ridiculous, Rebekka. Of course he is fine. You're overreacting. Calm down, for Pete's sake.

I felt tears pressing my eyes again and speeded up, hoping that there were no police in sight. Luckily, they were all at the hotel, parked by the front entrance, where they had put up a roadblock to keep curious passersby out. I parked down the street, then ran towards the crowd. I held up my press card and elbowed my way through the crowd. I spotted officer Jansson, who I had talked to the day before on the phone about the organ thefts. He was walking behind the roadblock. I called out to him. I knew him from way back, when I worked at a big national newspaper in Aarhus.

"Rebekka Franck?" He said and approached me. He signaled that I could come behind the police strip. "It happened again, huh?" I asked. "Any ID on the victim?"

The officer shook his head. "I haven't been up there yet. I just came in from Aarhus, so I don't know much. As far as I know, he is still on the operating table."

"But he must have had personal items like a wallet or something, right? They must have found his stuff in his room?"

"Probably. But you know how it is. They need to inform the relatives first, before they can tell the media."

"Naturally."

"You look worried." He suddenly said.

"I know someone who spent the night here last night. I guess I am just scared ..." I could hardly hold the tears back now. Officer Janssen saw it.

"My God, Rebekka. Are you alright?"

"I don't know. I just need to make sure it wasn't him. What room was the victim staying in?"

"Room 237."

39

AUGUST 2012

"WHO ARE YOU?"

The woman Henrik guessed was Barbara Rasmussen stared at him. "How did you get inside the building?"

Henrik grinned. "You don't know me, but I know a lot about you."

Barbara closed the door a little. "I'm not interested in buying anything."

"Oh, I'm not here to sell anything."

"So what do you want? Say, haven't I seen you somewhere before? Yes, I have. On TV. You're that kidney-guy. The guy who had his kidney stolen?"

"Guess I have become quite the celebrity, well we don't need any further introductions, then."

Barbara's eyes softened. She opened the door a little more. "I'm so sorry for what happened to you. Is that why you're here? Because you heard I was with Martin Damsgaard that night before ..."

Save the drama, bitch. It doesn't work on me. I see right through that little act of yours.

Henrik smiled compassionately and nodded. "Yes. That

is exactly why I'm here. I wanted to talk to you about that night."

Barbara shrugged and opened the door completely so Henrik could step inside her apartment. "I don't have much to tell, but if it'll bring you any comfort, then you're welcome."

Henrik put a hand to his chest. "Thank you so much. It means a lot to me. I have so many unanswered questions and no one to talk to about it." Henrik walked through the hallway and into the living room.

"Oh, I can understand how that must be hard," Barbara said behind him. "I feel like such a victim in this too. I'm so confused and I'm having a hard time sleeping at night since this happened. I mean, it was a close one for me too. I could as easily have been killed as well if I hadn't left during the night. I know I was lucky, but it still lingers with you, you know? Well, I guess you do know more than anyone, right? You must be frightened to death of going to sleep after this. Oh where are my manners? Do sit down in any of the chairs or on the couch. I'll make us some coffee. How do you take it?"

"Black." Henrik said and found an armchair to sit in. *As black as my soul.*

"Be right back. Make yourself at home," Barbara said and disappeared. Henrik could hear her rummaging in the kitchen. He looked at the paintings on the wall. Modern art had never been his thing. All just a lot of random strokes with the brush in different colors and then they dared to call it art. In Henrik's mind, artists had always been a bunch of freeloaders and parasites. It always enraged him when he read about the artists who received lifelong support from the Danish government. Was he really the only one who could see them for what they really were? Was he the only one to figure them out? It was so obvious that they simply just didn't want to work. They were lazy and didn't want to contribute to society, so now he had to pay for them through his taxes? Henrik had tried to write letters to the minister of culture and open letters to the newspapers about it, but no one seemed to care.

Henrik clenched his fist and hit the armrest of the chair. He restrained his anger and closed his eyes.

"Here we are," Barbara said and entered the living room.

Henrik opened his eyes and looked at her. She was quite beautiful even for a feminist. *Freaking man-hater, tell me why you still want your man to pay for dinner, huh? Why do you want him to hold the door for you if you're so freaking equal, huh? Let me show you who's in charge, I'll hold you down and fuck you back into your place. Treat you like a real woman.*

"I brought a little brandy to spice up the coffee," Barbara said with a smile. "It's not too early in the day for a little brandy, is it?"

"To hell with that," Henrik said and poured himself a big glass of brandy.

Barbara stared at his almost full glass, then poured herself a little on the bottom of hers. Henrik lifted his and spilled a little when it ran over the edge.

"To new beginnings," he said and their glasses clinked. Then he gulped down the entire glass.

Barbara stared at him and he could tell she was getting uncomfortable, when he put the empty glass down on the table and wiped his mouth with the back of his hand. Henrik smiled. "That hit the spot," he said. Then he leaned over and smashed his clenched fist into Barbra's face. "So did this."

The punch threw her backwards. Her nose was

bleeding and she was staring at him with great confusion. "What?" she mumbled and spat out a tooth.

"Now we can talk properly," Henrik said. "How many of you are there out there? Who is in charge?"

Barbara's eyes rolled in her head as she was trying to understand what Henrik had said. "What? What are you talking about? Why the hell did you hit me?" She tried to get up from the chair, but was too dizzy and fell backwards.

Henrik tried hard to relax, to hold back his anger. He felt like the paintings were staring at him, laughing at him, reminding him what a sucker he had been all of his life, working so hard paying his taxes and for what? So these talentless freeloaders could throw a few strokes with a brush on a canvas and call it art? Was that what they paid them to do?

"Please leave," Barbara stuttered. Her voice was shaking with fear. It annoyed Henrik even more. He tried to think of something nice. Like his third grade teacher had told him to when he felt that anger rise inside of him. *Just think of a beautiful meadow, think of the ocean, think of flowers, or your mom and dad. Whatever calms you down. Then count backwards from one hundred.*

Henrik did all of that right now. He saw the beautiful meadow, he pictured a waterfall in Hawaii, he imagined he was on a boat in the ocean fishing and drinking beer, he pictured the most gorgeous woman dancing in front of him wearing absolutely nothing at all. But still, he couldn't calm himself down.

"You need to leave now," Barbara said.

"I'm afraid I can't do that." Henrik said through gritted teeth. He poured some coffee from the pot and slurped it loudly.

"What ... What do you want from me? Why have you even come here?" Barbara asked.

"I want to know who you are working for. I've had my kidney stolen and I want to know what happened to it. Who has it?"

"I ..." Barbara tried to talk, but her mouth hurt. "I have no idea what you're talking about."

"Come ON! Don't you think I know? How stupid do you think I am? I know you're all working together. Don't take me for a FOOL. I know how it works. I have figured ALL of you out. All I want to know is what you have done with my stolen kidney. Where is it?"

Barbara was trying to get up from her chair again and this time she succeeded, holding on to the back of her chair. She reached out for the phone. Henrik watched her while laughing. Finally she managed to get the phone in her hand, when Henrik kicked it out of her hand and slammed his fist into her face once again. Barbara fell backwards, her head hitting the tiles so hard it sounded like a melon cracking. Henrik walked closer and looked at the blood that was running from the back of her head onto the white tiles.

What a mess.

40

JANUARY 2010

WHEN VALDEMAR TURNED FIFTEEN, he had long ago stopped asking if his father was going to come for his birthday. Not that Valdemar had forgotten about his father, no Anna knew he thought about him a lot and about how he had hurt his mother and him by leaving for another family.

And he hated him for it. The longing for his acceptance and love had turned into a resentment that Anna saw growing inside the eyes of her sweet young boy every day that passed. It blackened his insides, darkened his mind, and poisoned him with a deep, grieving sadness.

Valdemar would never tell her if she asked about it. He would say things like "Daddy didn't mean to hurt us, Mom. The other family needed him too."

Stuff like that that Anna knew he didn't mean. On the inside, his hurt grew deeper and deeper and for every day that passed, he became more and more isolated. Valdemar had taken a liking to computers and had taught himself hacking. Using nothing but his toes on the keyboard and the mouse placed underneath his table, he was able to hack his way into government sites and secret police files. In the beginning, he showed his mother proudly, but later he learned it was better to keep it a secret since Anna had freaked out and told him he would end up going to jail.

But she knew it hadn't helped that she told him that. He told her that he wasn't doing it anymore, but she knew he was. And she had no way of controlling it. Part of her was very impressed with his skills on a computer and in the garage where he still spent hours and hours creating inventions that Anna had never seen anything like. She had tried to threaten him with taking the computer away, but he knew she didn't mean it. The computer was his everything and, on Anna's modest salary, it was a big sacrifice for her to be able to buy it for him. She wasn't going to take it away and have wasted the money. So instead, she decided to try and keep an eye on what he was doing now and then. But truth be told, Anna had no idea what she was even looking for.

Valdemar was a lonely child. He didn't have any friends, but somehow Anna sensed that he didn't care much about it, about other children. She had a feeling he didn't like them much and found them to be childish and immature for him, since he had been a grown-up trapped in a child's body ever since he was no more than two years' old.

One Wednesday afternoon, a week after his birthday, Valdemar was sitting in his room, when Anna walked inside. He hurried up and hid something under the table by kicking it, but it was too late. Anna had seen it.

"What are you up to now, Valdemar?" she asked.

"Nothing," he sighed.

"Come on. I'm your mother. I know you. I can smell when you're up to something. Hand it over."

Valdemar picked it up with his feet and handed it to

Anna. She looked at it, but could make no sense of what it was. "A dry erase marker? What's so special about that?"

Valdemar looked guilty and Anna realized there was something inside of the marker. She pulled it out. It looked like a small circuit board and a lot of wires.

"What is this, Valdemar? Talk, or I'm definitely taking away the computer."

"You'll just get mad," Valdemar said.

"I'll try not to," Anna said. "Now speak up. What is this?"

"It's a key."

"A key?"

Valdemar nodded. He pulled out something else from under his desk with his feet and gave it to Anna. It looked exactly like a lock to a hotel door with a handle and everything. A small red light was blinking on top of it.

"What is all this?"

"It's a master key for all hotel room locks." Valdemar said.

"It's what?"

"I found a hole in the code to the Onity HT lock system for hotels. Approximately ten million Onity HT locks are installed in hotels worldwide. This accounts for over half of all the installed hotel locks and can be found in approximately a third of all hotels," he said.

"And this is one of those locks, I take it?" Anna asked.

"Yes. The Code key values consist of 24 bits of data and are used to gain entry to locks. A lock contains a guest code key value and, generally, one or more master code key values. Rather than programming the lock anew for every guest or when master keycards need to be made, a concept called *card cycling* is used. When a valid card is introduced to the lock, the lock's code key value is moved up to the value on the card. This allows the lock to automatically invalidate old cards when new ones are used. A 24-bit code key value has 16.7 million unique values, but this is divided by the lookahead plus one, as any card in that range will be valid. Thus if you have a lookahead of 50, the key space is reduced to only 328,965 values. With the lookahead set to the maximum, 255, the key space is reduced to only 65,536 values. While this means that, even in the worst case, you would need to try 32,768 cards in a door, on average, to open it, this introduces another problem. If two doors happen to be close enough in code key value that their lookahead values overlap, it's possible that a legitimate guest card intended for one door can open another door at the same property. When the doors are assigned initial code key values, these are separated by 1,000 to make this less likely. However, all doors are not created equally in a hotel, it's very likely that certain rooms will see higher turnover than others, leading to a situation where the code key values are likely to overlap ..."

Anna stopped Valdemar. "I have no idea what you're talking about, but this is not a good idea, Valdemar."

Valdemar looked down. He bent his head. Anna stared at the dry erase marker with curiosity. "So it works on all locks to all hotels, huh?"

Valdemar lifted his head. "Most hotels. Only those that use the Onity HT lock system."

"So how does it work?"

Valdemar smiled. With his feet, he grabbed the marker out of her hands. He put the circuit board inside and closed it on the back, then he grabbed the lock and put it on the table. Anna watched closely and couldn't help feeling a little proud of her son, yet terrified he would get himself in trouble with this.

"Now the Onity brand of key card locks most commonly

used in hotels have a power jack on the bottom that doubles as a 1-wire communications port ..."

"Simplify it, please," Anna said.

"Okay," Valdemar said. "See that small hole underneath the lock?"

Anna bent down and saw it. "Yes."

"Okay. Now I place the end of the marker down at the bottom here and give it a small push into the hole and then ... now look, did you see the lamp went from red to green?"

"'That's right, I saw that," Anna said, trying hard to not sound excited.

"Now you can turn the handle." Valdemar said.

Anna reached down and turned the handle.

"And the door is open."

Anna looked at her boy, then leaned over and kissed him. "You're a genius," she said. "Just promise me one thing."

"And that is?"

"Don't ever use it, alright?"

"It was never meant to be used. It was just an experiment."

41

AUGUST 2012

I WAITED NERVOUSLY FOR what felt like hours at the hospital before the doctor came out and told me Sune was in recovery.

"We managed to close him up. He's lost a lot of blood," the doctor said.

I was standing next to officer Jansson who had driven me to the hospital in his police car with blaring sirens and all.

"But he will make it?" Officer Jansson asked.

"It's too early to determine. The next twenty-four hours are crucial. We'll keep him under close observation."

"But he can live on without a spleen, right?" Officer Jansson asked.

"Yes. You can live perfectly well without your spleen. But because the spleen plays a crucial role in the body's ability to fight off bacteria, living without the organ makes you more likely to develop infections, especially dangerous ones like those that cause pneumonia, meningitis, and other serious infections. His own doctor will make sure the patient is given vaccinations to cover these bacteria."

I sat on a chair once the doctor was gone. I hid my face in my hands. "I can't believe this is happening. I can't believe it."

Officer Jansson sat next to me. He put his hand on my shoulder. "I'm sure he'll be alright."

"He has a son," I said. "I need to tell Tobias. He's back in Karrebaeksminde with his nanny."

Officer Jansson nodded. "Let me take care of that. I'll get the local police to contact them and have him transported here. Don't worry about that part."

Officer Jansson left the room talking on the phone. I took mine out and looked at it. Then I called Jens-Ole and told him. I hung up crying, then called Peter and told him not to say anything to Julie until I knew if Sune was going to live or not. Peter was very quiet and said nothing but *yes* and *no*.

Probably feeling guilty, I thought when I hung up.

The wait was terrible. My emotions ran amok. At one point I was crying for Sune and for the baby that might not get to know his father, then I was overwhelmed with guilt. If only I had been there. Maybe the organ thieves would have left him alone? Maybe I could have stopped them? Then I became angry. Angry at the thieves, at this cruel way to treat other people.

Officer Jansson soon returned. "Tobias is on his way in a police car. They told him his father was in the hospital, no details so far."

"I'll take care of him when he arrives," I said.

"Good." Officer Jansson sighed. "I'm afraid I have more bad news. There was another case last night."

"Two cases at the same time? What's going on here?" I asked.

He exhaled and touched his forehead. "I have no idea. This is crazy."

"What happened this time? Organ theft again? You think it was the same person?"

"'That's the strange part. It was a woman this time. All the others have been men," Officer Jansson said.

"Maybe it doesn't matter to them if it is a man or woman. An organ is an organ, right? On the black market, it probably doesn't matter. Or do you think they might be responding to orders? That someone places an order for a spleen from a woman to make sure it fits?" The thought was repulsive and made my stomach turn.

"I have thought about it. But the worst part about this one is that it was performed in her own home."

"What?" I asked.

"She lived in an apartment in Silkeborg, where she was found this morning by a friend she was supposed to go to Aarhus with today. The door wasn't locked, so the girlfriend walked right in when the woman didn't answer the door. She found her on the floor, blood everywhere."

"What organ had been stolen?"

"'That's the even stranger part. She had been cut open using one of her own kitchen knives and several organs had been cut loose, but none were missing. When the forensic team put her together it was all there. Some were on the floor and blood had spurted everywhere, like the person doing the cutting had gone berserk, but nothing was missing."

"That doesn't sound much like the other cases?"

"No not at all. In the three previous cases, the organ thieves have been very professional and even left the victims in ice with a note to tell them to call 1 1 2 when they woke up, if they woke up."

I felt sick picturing Sune sitting in the bathtub filled with ice-cubes. Who in their right mind could be this cruel?

"Maybe there are many of them out there? Maybe this one wasn't as controlled and professional as the others?"

"I don't know. It makes sense that there should be more of them since they struck at almost the same time last night in two places in the same town."

"Kind of makes you want to lock your door with extra locks, right?"

"And sleep with one eye open," Officer Jansson said. "I don't think I'll be able to sleep again before this case is solved."

42

AUGUST 2012

SUNE WOKE UP LATE in the afternoon and the doctor told me we could see him. Tobias had arrived and I had been reading to him for a long time to make sure he wasn't too scared.

"Daddy's going to be fine," I kept reassuring him.

Sune was very pale and could hardly look at us when we walked in. Tobias pulled free from my hand and stormed to him. He threw himself on top of him.

"Tobias! Be careful," I yelled.

Sune tried to smile, but was in too much pain.

"Hi buddy," he said hoarsely and put his arm around Tobias' back.

"Daddy. Daddy. I missed you so much. They say you were sick, what happened to you?"

Sune cleared his throat. "Well, I'll tell you all about it another day. When I'm feeling better, okay buddy?"

"Okay Daddy."

Sune closed his eyes for a few seconds. I hated to see him in pain like this. "How do you feel?" I asked.

"Like crap," he said. His eyes met mine, then he tried to smile. I walked closer and grabbed his hand.

"I'm so sorry," I said. "I'm so, so sorry."

"Well, you didn't do this to me, so I don't see why you should be sorry?" he said, trying hard to smile.

I felt so confused. Maybe it was just my hormones, but my emotions were going berserk. I was wondering if I should tell him, just blurt it out, but stopped myself. What if the child wasn't his? What if it was Peter's? That would only make things worse between us, it would kill him to know I was going to have a child with someone else.

"I'll be fine," Sune said.

I leaned over and kissed his forehead while a tear escaped the corner of my eye. "I was so scared I'd lose you," I whispered.

"Nah. You won't get rid of me that easily. Huh buddy?" He said, addressed to Tobias. "I'm like the weed in the yard."

I chuckled and studied his pale face. There were so many things I wanted to say to him and so many things I wanted to ask him, but I could tell he was exhausted.

"You need your rest," I said and kissed his forehead again. "I'll take Tobias down to the cafeteria and get him something to eat. What do you say, buddy? Maybe they'll have some ice cream for dessert?"

Tobias jumped down from the bed. As we were about to walk out of the room, he stopped and looked at his dad. "Will you be alright while we're gone, Daddy?"

Sune forced a smile, but he was already halfway asleep.

"He'll be fine," I said and grabbed Tobias' hand in mine.

Tobias didn't eat much of the food I bought for us and neither did I. Even the ice cream didn't taste right. Tobias kept turning his spoon in it.

"Better eat it before it melts," I said.

"He will be alright, won't he?" He suddenly asked.

"Yes, sweetie. He will. I know he will. These doctors are really skilled. They know how to take good care of your daddy. Don't you worry about that. I was thinking you might want to go with me back to the island tonight and maybe sleep in Julie's room with her?"

Tobias' eyes grew big and wide. "Really? We could do that?"

"We most certainly could and we will," I said and finished my soda. "Julie is going to be so excited to see you again. She has missed you a lot."

"And I've missed her. But what about dad? Will he be alright all alone?" Tobias asked.

"He is going to be just fine. He needs a lot of sleep and tomorrow he'll be feeling much better. Just you wait and see."

43

AUGUST 2012

HENRIK FENGER ASKED FOR another beer. The bartender took his glass and poured him one.

"And a whiskey," he said.

The bartender nodded, then gave him his drinks. Henrik looked at the foam on the beer and felt a pinch of sadness in his heart. He had no idea where to go. He couldn't go home to Roskilde since he was certain his wife wouldn't have anything to do with him and, frankly, he didn't want to go back anymore. Everything had changed the last couple of days. He had changed and there was no turning back anymore. Killing the two girls had left him excited, but not quite as satisfied as he wanted. He didn't understand what it was that was missing. He had gotten his revenge like he wanted, but still it left him unfulfilled somehow.

What was it that was missing? He wondered while gulping down the third whiskey since he entered the bar on the corner of the building where he had killed Barbara Rasmussen only a few hours earlier.

It dawned on him when he put the glass down and

moved on to the beer. He wanted to keep the buzz going all day. That was his plan so far. But he realized that he didn't feel as satisfied as he wanted to because he didn't feel like he had gotten the real bad guys. Killing the girls was fine, since they were both accomplices, but he knew now that there was no way they could have been alone on this. They had to have someone helping them, arranging it, maybe even planning it for them. Henrik sensed there had to be some kind of brains behind this, a leader somewhere behind all these attacks on innocent men. Some big fat woman who hated men and all they stood for.

Probably a dyke. A big fat ugly lesbo whom no man would ever touch.

Henrik turned the tall, slim beer glass between his fingers, wondering how he should get to the bottom of this, how he should find this fat leader who was pulling the strings on these girls and making them attack men, poisoning beautiful women into hating men.

Henrik lifted the glass and drank when he felt like he was being watched. He turned his head slowly and looked to his right side where a man was sitting in one of the booths. The man was grinning from ear to ear and very obviously staring at Henrik.

Henrik turned his head away and ordered another round of beer and whiskey, not paying any more attention to the strange man. These kinds of places often attracted some weirdos, especially at this hour of day. Henrik figured he was probably like a stray dog. If you ignore it, it'll go away.

The bartender gave Henrik a new round and he was about to drink the whiskey when a voice interrupted him. He turned his head with an annoyed sigh and saw the man from the booth was now sitting next to him at the bar.

"How was it?" The man asked.

Henrik shook his head. The man seemed even weirder up close. Couldn't he see Henrik wanted to be alone? "How was what?"

The man grinned again, then leaned closer. Henrik didn't want him this close and tried to lean in the other direction.

"The kill," the man whispered.

Henrik stared at the man. *Who the hell does he think he is, talking to me like that?*

"What are you talking about old man? I'm trying to enjoy a drink here. I'm really not looking for company."

As if he hadn't heard what Henrik said, the man leaned even closer. Then he sniffed Henrik. "I can still smell the scent of adrenalin on your skin. It's still fresh. How long has it been? A couple of hours since you killed her?"

"You're insane, do you know that?" Henrik said and drank from his whiskey, trying to ignore the strange man next to him.

"In that case, that makes two of us, then. We have a lot in common you and I. Who was she?"

"Who was who?" Henrik was getting really annoyed with this man and wondered if he should just get up and leave.

"The girl you killed."

Henrik almost choked on his whiskey. He looked at the man who was still grinning widely. "How do you know it was a girl?"

The man shrugged. "Just a lucky guess. Most men start out killing girls because they're an easier prey. I still kill only girls, but that's because I get a kick out of the power I posses over them. It never gets old."

Henrik looked in the direction of the bartender to make

sure he couldn't hear what they were talking about, then lowered his voice even further. "How did you know?"

"I can smell it from far away. I can always spot a killer in a crowd. Especially one who is new to it and has just killed. It's written all over your face. Takes one to know one."

"So you ... you're?"

"You got it. I spotted you from far away once you walked in here. I could see it in the look in your eyes, the way you moved, your hands were still shaking from the thrill."

"Well this girl had it coming. I was doing it for someone else, someone who couldn't defend himself, since the girl had killed him."

"Ah a hero, are we?" The man's voice became shrill.

"I don't know what I am," Henrik said.

"But I know," the man said. His voice whistled when he spoke. "You're a killer. Just like me."

"I'm nothing like you. I seek revenge. It's different."

"Oh the motive might be different, but you enjoyed it, didn't you? You liked to see the fear in their eyes, didn't you? That makes you no different than me. Besides you want to kill again. I can tell."

Henrik growled. Who was this strange man?

"You're new to it, I get it," the man continued. "You still tell yourself that you do it for a noble cause. But, take it from someone who has been in this for many years, you are not going to stop here. You're hooked. I see it in your eyes. You will be looking for that same feeling you felt when you did your first kill for the rest of your life. You will be longing for it at night. You'll wander the streets at night seeking for it, lusting to feel it again. Believe me. I know about these things. If you stick with me I might teach you a thing or two."

Henrik looked at the man again now with a new set of

eyes. Not because he suddenly liked the guy or because he really felt a kinship with him. No, but because he suddenly realized the man was right. Henrik had enjoyed killing the two girls and he did want to kill more. He wanted to kill all the women who were a part of this feminist group taking men's internal organs. He wanted to find the leader, the freaking dyke behind it all. And now he realized this strange man might be able to help him.

Henrik reached out his hand. "Henrik Fenger," he said.

The man shook his head. "No, No. Rule number one. You never give anyone your real name. Especially not someone like me. You come up with a name. Like me, I'm Karl Persson, how do you do?" He said and shook Henrik's hand.

"Make up a name, huh? Like what?" Henrik asked.

"My name belongs to a famous artist, a painter who is known worldwide for painting some very gruesome and vulgar pictures ... some of them even have strong cannibal-istic motives. I chose him because I see myself as an artist. Even if my art is never for anyone else to see or understand."

"I see," Henrik said. "So I could be like Dali or da Vinci?"

"Yeah, sure. Whatever you like."

Henrik nodded and finished his whiskey. "So tell me, are there more of your kind out there?"

44

JUNE 2011

IT STARTED JUST AS summer hit the country. At first it was nothing but a small insignificant cough, but then Valdemar lost his appetite.

In the beginning, Anna wasn't too worried since the boy never had eaten much and he didn't seem to grow much either. He was a handsome boy even if he was short and skinny, but suddenly, he started losing weight and that worried his mother.

One day he came down the stairs for breakfast as usual and his pants just slid right off him while he was walking. Anna almost dropped the pan with the scrambled eggs.

"What's going on with you lately?" she asked and helped pull up his pants before she served his breakfast.

Valdemar shrugged. He put his fork into the egg but only to push it around on the plate. Anna looked at him with worried eyes. Even his face had gotten skinnier.

"I think we should go and see doctor Kristensen," Anna said, as she ate her food.

"Do we have to?" Valdemar said.

"I think we need to. You're not eating and you're

coughing a lot. Maybe you have a light pneumonia or something. You don't seem to have a fever, but still, there is something going on. What do I know? You'll have to stay home from school today."

Valdemar smiled from ear to ear. Anna shook her head. "That doesn't mean you're not doing the work they did today. When we get back you'll call someone from your class and make sure you get all the work done that you missed today."

"Still a day off to me," Valdemar said. "It takes me ten minutes to do a day's school work. You know that."

Anna chuckled. "That's true."

"Plus, I'll have time to work on my game," Valdemar said.

"Game? What kind of game?"

"I've started developing a new computer game. It's pretty neat, if I say so myself. It's this world of blocks where you build your own house, or castle if you like and animals and stuff."

Anna smiled again. He always had something going on, the boy. *He is not sick. He seems fine. Maybe he just needs a day off.*

"I call it Mindskill," he said, smiling even wider than before.

"Sounds really great, honey," Anna said without really listening. Her head was filled with worried thoughts. "I'll call the doctor right away and schedule an appointment."

A week later, Anna was called into the doctor's office again. Doctor Kristensen was sitting behind his desk looking like he was the one who needed a vacation, Anna thought.

"Valdemar is not well, Mrs. Kragh," he said.

"What do you mean, he's not well? He is doing much

better now. The cough is getting better and yesterday he ate almost an entire burger. I think he is definitely improving."

"He might be, but not for long," the doctor said. "He'll soon start to go downhill fast."

Anna's heart stopped. "What do you mean go downhill?"

"Your son has Cystic Fibrosis. I don't know why we haven't caught this earlier, but he hasn't shown any symptoms up until now. I mean we both knew he wasn't growing much, but I figured it would kick in eventually."

"Cystic Fibrosis? What is that exactly?" Anna asked with a shivering voice.

"It's a lung disease. Actually a disease of the mucus and sweat glands. It affects mostly your lungs, pancreas, liver, intestines, sinuses and sex organs. It causes your mucus to be thick and sticky. The mucus clogs the lungs, causing breathing problems and making it easy for bacteria to grow. This can lead to problems such as repeated lung infections and lung damage."

"But what does this mean? How bad is it?"

Doctor Kristensen exhaled. "It's bad. In Valdemar's case, the disease has developed faster than usual. His lungs are heavily affected by this and I'm not sure how long he has left."

"How long he has left? What are you saying doctor? Is he ... will he ... die?"

The doctor exhaled deeply. "If he doesn't have a lung transplant within the next six months, I'm afraid so. Usually the patients might live till they're in their thirties, but not the way it is progressing in Valdemar. I'm sorry Mrs. Kragh."

"A lung transplant?" Anna asked. "How does that work?

"Well, we will get him on a list right away, but lungs are

not that easy to get. A lot of people are waiting for them right now, so the list is long and the donors few."

"What about me? Can I give him my lung?" Anna asked.

"You could. But not alone. Living lung donation requires two donors. One person giving one lobe, or a portion of their left lung, and the other giving a lobe of their right lung. The two lobes are transplanted into a single recipient. The donors' lungs must be the appropriate size and volume."

"So if I could find a second donor, we could save him?"

"Well there is always a risk of him rejecting the transplant, but it is the only thing that would be able to save him, yes. But you'd have to find one fast since Valdemar will only get weaker as the days pass by and he will need all his strength to be able to fight possible infections associated with the transplant."

Anna's mind was spinning with thoughts as she wondered who could make a possible donor for Valdemar.

"What about the father?" Doctor Kristensen asked. "Would he be willing?"

45

AUGUST 2012

THE KIDS WERE ECSTATIC. Tobias slept in Julie's room and the next morning, they both got out of bed and went downstairs to play on Julie's iPad without waking up anyone else in the house.

Peter was less excited about the whole thing. He barely spoke a word to me the night before and, in the morning, I heard him leave the bedroom without a word to me. I felt bad. No that's an understatement. I felt horrible. I felt like the worst scum on earth. I knew Peter was mad because I was more concerned about Sune than about him and our failing relationship. Because I worried more about Sune than about keeping my family intact. I knew that was how he felt. But it just wasn't that easy for me. I cared about Sune and I had to try and help him out. I loved Tobias and couldn't have just left him at the hospital.

I got out of bed and took a shower before I went downstairs. When I was done, I walked back to the bedroom and picked up my phone. Someone had left a message. I called my voice mail and listened to it. It was Jens-Ole.

"Hi Rebekka. I know you guys are busy and I realize it

might be quite insensitive given Sune's situation, but I wanted to let you know that the organ thieves have struck again, in case you hadn't heard. This time it was another woman in her apartment in Hasle. That makes it five cases in total these thieves have on their consciences. Three deaths and two survivors. Just wanted to fill you in. Let me know how you're doing and tell Sune we miss him."

I hung up and sat on the bed. Another woman in her apartment? What kinds of animals were these bastards?

I got dressed and walked downstairs where Tobias and Julie were laughing and playing on the iPad. "Mindskill again, huh?"

"Yeah, Tobias loves it too, Mommy. He knows how to get into a mode with dragons and butterflies and everything. And he knows cheat codes."

"He does? Wow." I said and walked into the kitchen. Peter was sitting in there all by himself eating toast with cheese.

I pulled out a chair next to him and sat down. "Is this how it's gonna be, Peter? You not talking to me?"

He sighed and wiped his mouth on a napkin. "I don't get it Rebekka. You come here to be with your family and then you're hardly with us."

"I can't help it that organ thieves are killing people and hurting one of my best friends and co-worker, can I?"

"I guess not. I just really wish Julie and I were higher up on your list of priorities."

I poured myself some coffee from the pot and sipped the cup. I didn't know what to say to him. To be honest, all I could think of was Sune and how he was doing.

"You're going to see him at the hospital today, aren't you?" Peter asked.

I sighed. "Yes, Peter. I am. He's seriously hurt. I'll take

the kids with me. Tobias needs to see his dad and Julie wants to be with Tobias. Look I'm trying my best here to please everybody."

"And you're doing a really good job," Peter said and smiled sarcastically. "You're making everyone happy except for me."

I closed my eyes. "Sometimes it's just not about you, Peter. Sometimes it's about people who have been hurt, people who were almost killed."

"People like Sune. Like your ex-boyfriend." Peter took another bite of his toast. It crunched between his teeth. The sound annoyed me just like he annoyed me immensely right now.

"Yes, I care about him still. Is that what you want to hear? Yes I still love him. There you go. Are you happy?"

Peter's face changed drastically. He got up from his chair.

"Peter don't ... It doesn't mean I don't love you as well. It's just not that simple for me. I can't just stop caring for a person like that. I'm not like you. I can't turn off my love like a faucet."

Right before he walked out the door to the kitchen, Peter turned around and looked at me. "Do what you want to today. Go see him. See if I care. I'll be in my studio painting."

"Peter ... don't be ..." But it was too late. He had left.

46

AUGUST 2012

KARL PERSSON SOON PROVED to be an interesting contact. After meeting at the bar, they had moved on to another bar, then another and, by nighttime, they were both so hammered they could hardly stand up straight.

Henrik crashed at Karl's place. A small basement in an old house from the seventies. He woke up on the couch with a serious hangover to the sound of the TV. He opened his eyes and looked straight into the eyes of Karl.

"Wakey wakey, hands off snakey," Karl grinned.

Henrik growled and sat up. With only one eye open he looked at the TV screen.

"What's going on?"

"You're famous," Karl shrieked. "They found your girl. Genius to make it look like it was the organ thief by the way."

Henrik growled again. He hadn't really thought of it as a cover up, but it was kind of effective, though he didn't like the idea of giving the feminists the credit or even more attention. That was what they wanted wasn't it? That was their purpose to it all, wasn't it? To get some lame point out to people. Exactly what the point to it all was, Henrik couldn't figure out, but they didn't fool him. As soon as he found their leader, he was going to ask her about it. He was going to get her to explain everything.

Right before he killed her.

"How do you know it wasn't the organ thieves?" Henrik asked.

"It's not his style. This one reeks of desperation, of frustration and anger. Plus the organ thief would never pick someone in her own home. He's only after businessmen on trips being unfaithful."

"How do you know? And why do you keep talking about it as if there is only one? The police seem to think it is an entire group."

Karl clapped his hands in excitement. "Because I know him."

Henrik opened both his eyes widely. "You what?"

"Yes," Karl said with a shrill voice. "I know the organ thief."

"How? How do you know him?" Henrik asked.

"I talk to him on a daily basis. Remember last night when you asked if there were others out there like you and me?"

Henrik remembered asking if there were others out there like Karl, not himself. *I'm not like you, you crazy imbecile.*

"Yes. Vaguely."

"Well, I answered that we often chatted with one another. That's how I know him and others just like him. We support each other, we help each other out."

Like a support group from hell or what?

"You do? How? How do you get in touch with this organ thief? How do you find him?"

Karl clapped his hands again and jumped in excitement. He pulled out an old laptop and placed it in Henrik's lap. "His name is Bill Durgin. He's new to the chat forum, but I speak with him almost every day. He always writes right before a kill, when he is sitting in the hotel bar waiting for his victim. He especially looks for businessmen who pick up women and bring them back to hotels. If you look at the screen you'll see his latest writing."

Henrik looked at the screen. Karl had been writing in the chat room all morning while Henrik was still asleep. Someone called Alex Andreyer had answered. And then there was one message from the one called Bill Durgin. Henrik read it.

I didn't kill those women. Someone out there is impersonating me.

Don't be so angry about that, a Thomas De Quincey answered. *It just means you have the public's attention. You are someone people want to be. Someone people out there are trying to copy. Only the biggest artists are being copied. Be proud.*

"Who's that Thomas De ... Quincey?" Henrik asked.

"He's the one who came up with the whole thing. He created the secure chat room. We were shut down a month or so ago when the police discovered us because of some lunatic named Allan Witt who went berserk, but Thomas created a new page for us, even more secure than the first. He's the real genius here. His art by far excels any of what the rest of us are doing."

"So, he is the leader? He is the one telling you what to do?" Henrik asked.

"Well, not exactly. He has set up some rules for us to follow so we won't get caught. He helps us out to become all we can be and not get stopped by the police. He helps us with details when we come to him and ask for his help. He makes sure we don't screw up. He has killed more people than any of us. We draw on his expertise, so to speak."

"What's in it for him? Why is he doing it?" Henrik asked.

"We donate a sacrifice to him," Karl said. On TV an officer was talking to the reporter in front of Barbara's apartment.

"A sacrifice? What kind of sacrifice?"

"We donate something. It can be the body of our first kill, or a body part, or photographs or something like that. But it has to be something big. Something that characterizes us as killers and why we do it."

Just when I thought the world couldn't get any crazier?

Henrik rubbed his forehead wondering what he had gotten himself into. He scrolled the chat and stopped at a message send by Karl earlier in the morning. He read it while Karl watched TV, grinning from ear to ear.

Caught myself a little something last night. Will have fun with him for a while, then cut him to pieces and eat him for dinner tonight. My first male. Thought it was about time I progressed. Wish me luck.

AUGUST 2012

Sune looked at lot better when we arrived at the hospital. He was sitting up when Tobias and Julie ran to him and crawled into his bed.

"Easy there kiddos. He just had surgery," I said.

Sune chuckled and hugged the both of them.

"Wow, you look great," I said and placed a bouquet of flowers in a vase next to him. "You even have some color in your cheeks again."

"I feel a lot better. How has he been?" He said and touched Tobias' hair.

"I think he is fine. A little worried last night and found it hard to fall asleep, but being with Julie helped a lot, I think."

"I'm fine Daddy," Tobias said. Julie laughed, acting silly, and Tobias copied her.

I smiled, enjoying watching them together again. I missed it.

"Those two have been inseparable ever since I brought him home."

Sune looked at me. Our eyes locked. I felt warm. A stirring grew inside of me. "Thank you," Sune said. "Thank you for all you have done."

"It's no problem, really. It's nothing. The least I could do."

Sune grabbed my hand and pulled me closer. "I don't think it's nothing."

Julie jumped down from the bed and pulled my shirt. "Mommy. Can Tobias and I go out in the hallway and play Mindskill on your phone? I want to show him something."

I looked at Sune. "Don't you think Tobias wants to be with his dad a little?"

"It's okay," Sune said. "Let them have their fun."

"Okay then. Just don't leave the floor, alright?"

They both promised. I gave them my phone and they stormed out the door. I pulled a chair close to Sune and sat down.

"So I was planning on calling officer Jansson later today," I said. "You know to hear how they're doing on catching those who did this to you and all. Did you hear there was another case?"

Sune looked at me, then shook his head. "No I've been kind of busy with getting well and all."

"Of course, no, I'm silly. It was another woman. That makes it two women who were both killed in their own apartments and three men who were attacked in hotel rooms. It's weird I think. There is something I don't quite understand. Why bother with the hotel rooms where you could easily be spotted if you might as well go inside someone's apartment and take their organs. And another thing, in both cases with the women, the attacker didn't take any of their organs at all. He just opened them up and cut the organs loose. In the second case, the body had been more chopped with a knife than cut professionally. It is very unlike what happened to you and the kidney-guy." I paused and looked at Sune who was avoiding my eyes.

"I'm sorry," I said. "I'm being insensitive here."

"No. I like to hear you talk, but ..."

I interrupted him. "I was thinking that maybe you could help me learn more by hacking into the police files? Or maybe ... no you're too tired."

Sune sighed and looked at me. "If it's important to you, I'll do it."

I grabbed my laptop and put it on Sune's lap. "Well it's not only important for me, it's important for you too."

I flipped through a magazine while he let his magic fingers dance across the keyboard.

"There you go," he said. "I'm in. Now I'll take a nap if you don't mind."

"No go ahead. I'll just go through it."

Sune turned around to try and sleep.

"This can't be right," I said.

Sune turned and looked at me.

"I'm sorry," I said. "You're trying to sleep. I'll be quiet."

He forced a smile. "No. I can tell you are dying to tell me what it is Rebekka. Go ahead."

I jumped up from the chair and put the laptop on his lap again. "See this? Look at the names here and there."

"They are the same. So what?" Sune asked.

"These are the names of the women who were killed and the women sleeping in the hotel rooms with two of the victims. Apparently, the rumors were right about Henrik Fenger. He wasn't alone as he claimed to be. But, don't you see? They are the same two women."

Sune looked at me. "So what do you think this means?"

"Well, it's strange, isn't it? It can hardly be a coincidence, can it? The same two women?"

Sune shrugged. "Who knows?"

I grabbed the laptop in my hands and scrolled more, then opened a new file and gasped.

"What?" Sune asked.

"The body of Martin Damsgaard has gone missing."

"Excuse me?"

"You know, the guy who died after having his liver taken. Look here," I said and showed him the screen. "The police believe someone broke into the forensic department in Aarhus where he was being examined and stole the body of Martin Damsgaard a couple of nights ago. There was no sign of breaking and entering, though." I paused and thought for a second. "Hm, there was no sign of breaking and entering in the apartments of the women either."

"It's all very interesting, Rebekka, but ..."

"I wonder if there is a connection to the disappearance of the bodies of the kings from the churches?"

"Why on earth should there be a connection to that?" Sune sounded tired now. He rubbed his eyes.

"I don't know, but it's strange right?"

Sune exhaled deeply. "Maybe it's just me because I'm really tired, but I honestly don't care, Rebekka."

"Don't care? How can you say that? These people attacked you while you were asleep. They sedated you and took your spleen. They almost killed you. You almost bled to death. How can you not care?"

Sune closed his eyes. "I just don't. Not anymore. It's not worth it."

"Not worth it? Hello? Where is the real Sune and what have you done with him?"

"Very funny, Rebekka," Sune said with a tired voice.

"Don't you want to catch these thieves or at least help

the police catch them? Don't you want them put away for what they did to you?" I asked.

Sune looked at me. There were tears in his eyes, but he tried to repress them. "Don't you see it doesn't matter anymore? All I care about right now is getting well. And then I want to take my son and go home."

I couldn't believe my own ears. What was going on? This was so unlike him. "But we are so close. I feel that we are so close to finding who is behind all this."

"Rebekka. I really don't want to talk more about this. And I don't want you to come and pretend to be interested in me or pretend to be caring or whatever it is you're doing here."

"What I am doing here? I'm trying to help you out. I do care about you, Sune. You know I do," I said.

Sune looked at me. The look in his eyes felt like a knife to my heart. "Who are you kidding here? Who are we kidding? I'm sick of this. I'm sick and tired of this life going back and forth with you, thinking one moment that you want to come back, knowing in the next that you never will. Do you think this is easy for me Rebekka? Do you think it is easy for me to be around you constantly?"

"What are you saying?"

"I get that you have a hard time choosing between me and Peter so I'm going to make it easy for you. Leave and don't come back. I'm going to quit my job at the newspaper and go away with Tobias, leave Karrebaeksminde. There, I made the choice for you. Now leave."

48

JULY 2011

ANNA TRIED HARD TO hold back her tears. She was sitting outside Michael's office waiting for him while his secretary was on the phone. She looked down at the 60GB memory stick in her hand that she so sincerely hoped would help save the life of her beloved son.

Valdemar had gotten a lot worse just in the last month, since Anna had received the news from the doctor and waited to gather the courage to face Michael for the first time since the day he left to be with his other family.

Back then, he had offered to help them financially, but Anna had refused to take any of his money. And, up until now, they had done fine without him; to be frank, life had been much easier without him. It was only the hurt in her son's eyes that reminded her that Michael had once been in her life. Back when he left, she had thought she would never see him again, especially never be asking anything from him again.

It was like life was laughing at her right now. It was the cruel irony of destiny that she now had to beg him for something again. It felt so humiliating, so demeaning.

Anna took in a deep breath to calm herself down. When she was about to leave the house, she went upstairs to say goodbye to Valdemar who had spent most of the week in bed. He was lying on his back coughing heavily as she entered. She kneeled next to him fighting her tears.

"I'm leaving now, sweetie. Wish me luck."

Valdemar had tried to laugh, but it ended in another cough attack. The doctor had told them he only had ten percent of his lung capacity left now. Valdemar looked at her while breathing heavily. Oh, how she hated that sound, that wheezing, hissing sound he made when he gasped for air. All night she would lie awake listening to him in the room next door, worrying about him, thinking at least he was still breathing and fearing the day the sound stopped and all she would wish was for it to start again.

"Why are you going there anyway? It's a waste of your time," Valdemar said, out of breath. He paused and took in a deep breath. "He's not going to say yes. What has he ever done for us?"

"I know it's a long shot. But, he is, after all, your father. I loved him once, remember? Enough to marry him, enough to have a child with him."

Valdemar coughed and wheezed. "He's a worthless bastard, that's what he is."

"I know, sweetie. But he's our only hope right now."

Valdemar breathed with trouble. His nostrils moved when he breathed in air. "I have something I want you to bring to him," he said. "I want you to show him my game." Valdemar held up a memory stick in the air with his toes and handed it to Anna.

Anna looked at her boy and stroked his hair gently. Her handsome, sweet boy. All he ever wanted in life was for his daddy to accept him, to love him. Still now, as a teenager, sick with a deadly disease, that was all he could think about.

"It's all on this. Promise me you'll show it to him, will you?"

"Of course, sweetie." Anna leaned over and kissed his forehead. "I promise you I will."

Valdemar closed his eyes to rest. Anna stayed and watched him breathe. A tear fell from the corner of her eye and rolled across her cheek. Oh how she wished she could just give him both of her lungs. She had pleaded with the doctor to take hers and give them to him, but the doctor had said it wasn't legal, that she would die. Anna had said it didn't matter, but still, the doctor refused.

"Mr. Jacobsen is ready for you now, Mrs. Kragh," the secretary said and pulled Anna out of her reverie.

"Thank you," Anna said and walked towards the door. With a deep breath she put her hand on the handle and pulled it down.

Michael wasn't even looking up when she entered.

"Hello Michael," she said.

49

AUGUST 2012

KARL PERSSON WAS STILL GRINNING when Henrik closed the lid of the laptop.

"So, aren't you proud?" he asked and pointed at the TV where they were still talking about the death of Barbara Rasmussen. "You're all over the news. Gives quite the kick, doesn't it?"

Henrik shrugged and put the laptop away. "I guess."

"Aw, come on. Don't be so modest. I know how it feels. Usually I make sure no one ever finds the bodies, but it happened to me once that my kill made the news. I remember feeling like the king of the world. The entire country was appalled by what I had done. Everybody was talking about the dismembered body of a teenage girl that had been found in a dumpster. Chopped into small pieces. The public ate it all raw. Fascinated and repulsed at the same time, they were all glued to the TV. That was back in the late eighties, back when a killing like that was a huge thing and would be in the news for weeks. Nowadays, it drowns in all the other bad stuff. You'll have to do some real nasty stuff to impress the news. Like the organ story. That's new. Never been seen before. I tell you, this Bill Durgin is a genius."

Infuriated by Karl's last sentence, Henrik stared at the screen. A reporter was talking to the anchor while yellow signs were flashing in the bottom *BREAKING NEWS - Woman killed in her home by the organ thieves last night.*

Henrik didn't care one bit about all this. All he kept wondering was how he was going to get out of this apartment alive. This lunatic was dangerous and, right now, planning on killing him and chopping him into pieces. Henrik looked around and saw no knives or other deathly weapons. Karl was still grinning like someone who had just won the lottery.

"We should celebrate your newfound fame," Karl said and went into the kitchen.

Henrik looked at the front door and wondered if he should just make a run for it. But where was he going? He looked around the small basement. He could also choose to stick around for a while.

"I have beer," Karl said and showed up carrying a six-pack. He handed one to Henrik.

"Cheers," Henrik said.

They drank. Karl emptied his, but Henrik only took a small sip. He still felt sick from yesterday's drinking and he wanted to stay alert.

"So, are you hungry?" Karl asked when he was done with his beer. He wiped his mouth with the back of his hand.

"A little," Henrik answered.

Karl smiled from ear to ear. "Me too." He stared at Henrik, like he was sizing him up. "I thought I might chop something up for us. Make a stew or something. One of those that need to simmer for hours in a delicious sauce. What do you say?"

Henrik took another sip of his beer. It tasted suddenly strange and he wondered if Karl had put something in it. Or was he just imagining things? Was Karl staring at him with lust in his eyes? Lust for the kill? Was it really him that he had written about in the chat or could it be someone else? Could it have been an old message?

Of course it was you, you idiot. Don't be a fool.

Henrik smiled. "I say it sure sounds great. What kind of stew?"

"I was thinking either heart in crème sauce, or I could do something completely different, how about pan fried liver, or kidney flambé? I once made boiled, smoked tongue, now that was really something. What do you think?"

"I think it all sounds very delicious. It's hard to choose really. I'm fine with any of it," Henrik said. His hands were sweating. It was hard to hold on to the beer. "Or we could just call for a pizza?"

"Oh, but that's so boring, now isn't it? So ordinary," Karl said and took a step forward.

Henrik nodded and pulled back. "I guess."

"So, what'll be then?" Karl asked. "The guest decides."

"I'm really not that hungry anymore."

"Oh, that's a shame. Good thing that I've been known to have an appetite for two then."

Henrik was sweating heavily and had clammy hands. Karl was approaching him slowly now, looking at him like he was studying him closely.

"You know, I did wonder for a long time what to do with a man once I killed him," he said. "I mean, women I know how to handle. I rape them, then kill them. But why kill a man I kept asking myself? Besides the rush of the kill, what will I get out of it? Last night, I kept wondering and wondering until I came up with the idea. Why not COOK them?"

As Karl spoke the last words, he jumped towards Henrik and grabbed him around his neck with both hands and started squeezing. Henrik gasped for air and tried to fight Karl off. He took the bottle in his hand and hit it hard against Karl's head until it shattered. Karl cursed and let go of Henrik, who was now standing with a broken bottle in his hand. Karl was holding a hand to his head when Henrik swung the broken bottle towards his face and cut him. Karl screamed, then tried to punch Henrik, but Henrik grabbed his fist mid-air, and bent it backwards, until Karl screamed. Henrik stared at the squirming Karl who was bleeding from his face. Henrik was breathing heavily and feeling the anger rising in him again. It felt incredible. *He* was like the incredible Hulk, bending Karl's arm backwards, till he heard it crack and Karl screamed in pain. When Henrik let go of the arm again, it was dangling from Karl's shoulder, the cracked bone poking out through the skin. Now it was Henrik who was grinning as he approached Karl puffing himself up like the Hulk, feeling how the anger allowed his muscles to grow and his strength to increase.

As he lifted his fist and punched Karl hard in the face again and again, knocking out teeth and breaking his lip, he realized that Karl had been absolutely right.

Henrik did get a kick out of killing people. It was his fix and from now on he would never be able to live without it again.

AUGUST 2012

I was stunned. Heartbroken beyond speech as I drove with Julie back to the island. The winds had picked up a lot now and leaves were flying everywhere, even branches kept falling from the trees as we passed them. On the radio, they kept talking about the storm that was supposed to approach tonight and sweep across the country during the next couple of days. They expected roads to be closed due to falling trees and possible flooding and asked people to stay inside and only go out if absolutely necessary.

The trip across the lake was nasty with the churning water, but we made it to the dock and walked across the island towards the big mansion with our clothes flying in all directions.

"Mommy I'm scared," Julie shrieked, when the wind pushed her sideways. I grabbed her hand and pulled her closer. I held her tight and helped her push her way against the strong wind. When we were closer to the house, Peter came storming out and grabbed the both of us and helped us get back inside.

"I saw you from the window," he said. "You should have called me and told me you were on your way back. I had no idea you were out in this horrible weather."

I took off my jacket and put my bag on a table. I had no idea what to say to him or to anyone for that matter. I still had a hard time comprehending that Sune never wanted to see me again and that my daughter had been deprived of her best friend. I was heartbroken, to put it mildly.

"Are you okay?" Peter asked as he tucked my hair behind my ear. "Is Sune alright?"

"Sune is fine," I said feeling the tears press from behind my eyes. Peter saw it and pulled me close. He hugged me for a little while and it felt really good. I wanted so badly to cry, but didn't want the questions that were bound to follow. I simply couldn't tell Peter why I was this upset. It would hurt him. I wondered what to do next and felt so hopeless.

What about the baby? What if it is Sune's?

"Let's go get some hot chocolate," Peter said. He looked at Julie who nodded with a smile.

"That sounds great," I said.

We went into the kitchen and sat at the table while Peter made the hot chocolate for us. I enjoyed watching him in the kitchen.

"So Sune is going to be alright?" Peter asked.

"That's what the doctors say, yes," I said.

"And then they're moving," Julie said. "It's so unfair."

Peter looked at me. "They're moving?"

"Yes. Sune told me they're leaving Karrebaeksminde as soon as he gets back. He told me he will be leaving the paper as well. Guess he wants to move on."

"Well that is great news," Peter said.

"No it's not," Julie said.

"Try to hide your enthusiasm just a little, Peter," I said.

"No, of course it's not great that you're losing your best friend, sweetie," he said and served the hot chocolate for us. He put whipped cream on top. "But you'll make a lot of new friends soon."

"Not one like Tobias," Julie said.

"No, but another one. Maybe even a better one, right? Maybe a little girl who likes horses just like you?" Peter tried again. He sat next to Julie while I sipped my cocoa, hoping it would help cure my sadness. "Look at it this way," Peter said. "When we get back, you have a lot to look forward to. Your mom and dad will probably move in together again and you'll get your family back."

Julie smiled and leaned her head on her dad's shoulder. "I would like that," she said. "But what about grandpa? Who's going to take care of him?"

"We'll hire a nurse," Peter said.

That's your answer to everything, isn't it Peter? Just hire someone to fix it.

"We will visit him all the time," I said. "And we'll find a house close by."

"Yeah. But who am I going to play with?" Julie said. "I loved to play with Tobias."

Peter looked at me and smiled, then he looked back at Julie. "Well your mom and I just might have an answer for that too," he said. "See, right now your mommy is carrying a little brother or little sister in her stomach and when he or she comes out, you'll always have someone to play with. Isn't it wonderful?"

I spurted out a mouthful of hot cocoa on the table.

"We're having a baby?" Julie shrieked.

Peter smiled and nodded.

I stared at him.

"What?" He asked. "I found your pregnancy test in the garbage in the bathroom. We had to tell her at some point. This seemed like the perfect time."

51

JULY 2011

"WHAT A SURPRISE TO SEE YOU HERE," Michael said. "What can I do for you?"

Anna sighed. The nervousness and anxiety made her stomach hurt. She looked into Michael's eyes, looking to see if she could spot the man she had once loved and who had loved her.

"Valdemar is sick."

Michael shrugged. "So take him to the doctor."

"No not like that. He is really sick. Seriously ill. He has Cystic Fibrosis."

"So what?" Michael said and looked down at his papers. "Listen, I'm really busy these days. In case you haven't heard, our company is in big financial trouble, the economic crisis has made people stop buying toys for their kids. We need something major to pick us up. I have to go through all these new products to find that one thing, that one big best-seller that can help us get back on top. If I don't, I'm fired. So you can understand why I'm trying to have you get to the point here. What is it you want from me?"

"I want a part of your lung," Anna said.

Michael dropped his paper. Now she had his attention. "You want what from me exactly?"

"Valdemar needs a lung transplant or he'll die. His lungs are below ten percent in capacity as it is. And it's going downhill fast now, the doctor says. He keep getting infections and the doctor says he won't be able to pull himself through them for much longer. His body simply can't keep fighting them. So he needs new lungs. They need two donors. I'll be one and I'm asking you to be the other. They won't take your entire lung, just a part of it, or a lobe as they call it. I'm no expert but I know a person has five lobes and they'll only be taking one out. One from you and one from me. You'll naturally have to undergo a series of medical and psychological tests first."

Michael stared at Anna like she was insane. "This is a joke, right? This is you getting back at me for leaving you, right?"

Anna shook her head. "No. I'm serious here Michael. Valdemar will die if we don't help him."

Michael exhaled and leaned back in his leather chair. He was quiet for a long time, while a million thoughts ran through Anna's mind.

Come on, Michael. Step up for once. Show the boy you're not a bastard. Be human for once.

Michael looked at Anna. He shook his head and leaned forward.

"Michael. This is important. This is a matter of life or death for our son. Don't you dare ..."

But it was too late. Michael had made up his mind. Anna could see the determination in his eyes. They had the same cruelty to them as they had on the day he saw Valdemar for the first time in the hospital. "The boy was a mistake from the beginning, Anna. You know how I feel about him. Maybe this is just nature's way of sparing him a horrible life. You know he will never be able to do any of what other kids do. He will never be able to live a normal life. Who would hire him? Who would marry him, huh? A sick man with no arms? Do you think he is going to provide grandchildren for you, huh? How should he be able to do that? Who would want to be with him? Is he going to live with you for the rest of his life?"

Anna couldn't believe what he was saying. The cruelty, the heartlessness. It was unbearable. "What are you saying, Michael?"

"I'm saying, I think it is for the best if he dies. I know it's going to sound cold-hearted, but that's how I feel. It would give you a chance to finally move on. You've been stuck with him for way too long. He was never meant to live, Anna."

"How can you be so cruel?"

"Nobody likes to hear the truth, but that's all it is. The boy is useless."

Anna lifted her hand and threw the memory stick on the desk. "You see this? On this memory stick is a game, a computer game that Valdemar has created for the sole purpose of impressing you. And that's just one thing. Our house is packed with inventions made by him. I tell you Michael, the boy is a genius. He is NOT useless. He is brilliant, and if you can't see that then you're fucking blind."

Anna was standing in front of Michael's desk now, snorting in anger. When she saw no change in Michael's eyes, she turned around and left. Through the open door to his office, Anna heard Michael yell:

"It's the best for him, Anna. I'm doing him a favor don't you see?"

52

AUGUST 2012

HOURS HAD PASSED. There was blood all over the floor. Henrik even had it on his face and all over his clothes from beating Karl. Now, he wasn't moving anymore and Henrik took a break. Panting, he blew on his hand, which was sore from the beating. He looked at Karl who still wasn't moving and realized he wasn't breathing either.

Henrik shrugged, then went into the kitchen and found a big knife. He started cutting Karl open and took out his organs, one after another, making it look like organ thieves once again, in case they found his body. Then he found some black garbage bags and put all the organs inside of it. He tried to cut off the right arm, but it was way too hard and the knife wasn't sharp enough. How Karl had been able to chop his victims into pieces, Henrik didn't understand.

But it wasn't his thing, he discovered. It was way too difficult. Instead he put the remains of Karl on the rug and rolled him inside of it. He really didn't care what happened to Karl's body, but he didn't want to leave it in the basement, since Henrik was planning on crashing there for a couple more nights.

So, Henrik pulled the rug into a small closet where he placed it leaning against the wall and placed the black bag of organs next to it, then closed the door and locked it.

There. Out of sight out of mind.

Henrik took a shower and put on some of Karl's clothes. Luckily, they were almost the same size. He looked at himself in the mirror and thought he could easily be mistaken for Karl. Henrik went back into the living room and looked at the old laptop on the coffee table. Then he picked it up. Karl was still logged into the chat room and someone had written to him.

Karl are you there? The one called Andreyer had asked half an hour ago.

Henrik smiled to himself, then wrote. *Yes. I'm still here.*

A few minutes passed before there was another reply. *Did you make your kill?*

Henrik chuckled as he wrote: *I did.*

How do you feel? Was it good?

It was amazing. Much better than expected.

Henrik found a new beer and sat down on the couch with the TV still on in the corner of the basement. Some British series was showing. He looked at the screen and waited for an answer.

Suddenly, a small line on the screen said *Bill Durgin joined the chat.* Henrik almost choked on his beer and sat up straight. Bill Durgin. This was the one he was looking for. He was the one who had taken the organs, Karl had said. Was he the one who had taken Henrik's as well? Karl had said he was the only one doing this, but that would mean Henrik had killed those girls in vain?

Well not in vain. They were stupid bitches who no one was going to miss anyway. But, he was willing to admit that maybe they hadn't been a part of some greater feminist conspiracy after all. That much he would give them. But they deserved to die. Just like Karl deserved to be killed. Henrik was still doing the world a favor. He was still a hero, of sorts. Not one who would ever be honored for his accomplishments. No, as a matter of fact, he *was* a little like the incredible Hulk. Misunderstood, but still a hero. And so what if he accidentally killed a few innocent people along the way? The end justified the means after all, didn't it? Well, something like that. Henrik didn't feel guilty or bad for killing the girls. He was way beyond feelings like that. Killing them had made him feel better and killing Karl had been the best sensation he ever had. That justified anything, in his mind.

What's up, Bill? He wrote. *Chosen a new victim yet?*

Seconds passed by while Henrik finished his beer. Finally the cursor blinked and Bill wrote:

Looking at him as we speak. He's eating Soft Tofu soup.

53

AUGUST 2012

I WAS FURIOUS WITH Peter and ran upstairs, pretending to have to go to the bathroom. I was walking back and forth in the bedroom not knowing what to do. He knew about the pregnancy, and now he had told Julie about it as well? Julie was so exited and apparently so was Peter. But I wasn't. I had no idea what to do.

I sat on the bed and felt my stomach. Yes there was already a small bump there, one that only I could see, but it was there. It was really happening. But what if the child wasn't Peter's? Did I pretend it was? Did I just decide it was probably his and then say nothing to Sune? After all, he had told me he wanted out of my life completely. That he never wanted to see me again. I felt my stomach and realized I really wanted this baby. I was already looking forward to seeing it, to holding it in my arms. Who cared who the father was? And, I knew Peter would be a great father, just like he was to Julie. But could I live without knowing for sure?

I shook my head with a sigh. Of course I couldn't. Sune wanted a second child more than anything. I couldn't deprive him of it. He had to know. I would have to ask him to take a paternity test at some point. That was the right thing to do.

But how was Peter going to react to that? Would he resent the child because he wasn't the father?

My head was spinning with thoughts and worries when my cell phone suddenly rang. I looked at the display and realized it was my sister.

"Hello?" I said.

"Rebekka. I ..."

She sounded upset. My heart stopped.

"What's the matter? Is it something with dad?"

"He ... I came to check in on him and found him. He was lying on the floor in the kitchen. He had fallen and hurt his head. Rebekka, you have to come home. I'm afraid it's serious. We're at the hospital now. They say he had another stroke."

"Oh my god. I'm coming right away," I said and hung up.

I shoved my things into my suitcase and stormed downstairs. "What's going on?" Peter asked.

"Julie, go upstairs and start packing your things. We have to go back to Karrebaeksminde," I said.

Peter approached me. "Hey, what's going on?"

"We're leaving. It's my dad. He's in the hospital. He fell and hurt his head. We have to get back."

Peter clenched his jaw. "Now?" He asked. I could tell he was restraining his anger. "Does it have to be right now? I mean we were just finding each other as a family here. We were having a moment."

"Are you insane?" I asked. "My dad hurt himself. I have to be there. He had a stroke."

"I hear you loud and clear there, Rebekka. But I'm asking does it really have to be like RIGHT now?"

Peter was looking at me in a strange way and yelling certain words, making him sound like a crazy person.

"What do you mean?"

"I mean there is always some sort of emergency with you, isn't there? Couldn't we, for once, just NOT run to it? Couldn't we, for once, let someone else handle it?"

"No. Peter it's my dad we're talking about here ..."

"Yes, and yesterday it was your ex-boyfriend we were *talking about here,*" Peter said imitating my voice. "When is it going to stop, huh?"

"It's my dad," Peter. "This is more important than anything else, than anyone else, even you, Peter."

Peter's head tilted from side to side while he stared at me with manic eyes. *"More important than anyone, even you Peter,"* he repeated, mocking me.

"What's going on here, Peter? What is this?"

Peter looked at me grinning, then lifted his hand and slapped me across the face so hard I fell to the floor. He was still smiling when I looked up at him holding a hand to my hurting cheek.

"THIS is what is going on here, Rebekka. I'll tell you what is going on here. You're not going anywhere. You're staying here with me. That's what's going on. I'm taking back control."

"Taking back control, what the hell are you talking about Peter?"

"What the hell are you talking about Peter," he copied me.

My heart was racing and my face hurt badly. I felt so confused. Julie came down the stairs. "Mommy? What's going on? Daddy?"

Peter turned on his heels and smiled at Julie. "Oh nothing sweetie. Your mom and I are just discussing a little matter. Nothing to worry about. Just go back to your room and unpack. We're all staying here."

"Julie," I yelled. "We need to get out of here."

Peter turned quickly and looked at me. "And just how do you suppose you'll be able to do that, huh? There is a raging storm outside and there is no way you'll make it to the other side in that tiny boat of ours ... if you make it that far."

I stood up. Peter grabbed my arm and held me tight. "Peter. You're hurting me."

"Well that's kind of the point, Rebekka."

"Mom?" Julie sounded scared.

"Go to your room Julie," Peter said. "I'll be up to tuck you right in."

"But ... it's not nighttime yet?"

"Just GO!"

Julie stormed back up the stairs with a whimper, while Peter tightened his grip on my arm. Then he started pulling me towards the stairs as well.

"What are you doing Peter?"

"I have something to show you, dear Rebekka. Something I've been wanting to show to you for a very long time."

54

AUGUST 2012

ANNA WAS LOOKING AT herself in the mirror of the hotel bathroom. In the room next door, she could hear Michael chatting with the woman he had just picked up in the bar downstairs after his dinner in the restaurant. Now they were going at it and she recognized his moans and dirty talk from back when she had been with him. Sex with Michael had always been rough and she didn't miss it one bit. She looked at the iPad, then wrote something in the chat room.

Love the thrill of waiting.

I know, Andreyer wrote back. *It's the anticipation, the expectation of what is about to happen that is so exiting. But not as exiting as the actual kill. Enjoy it Bill.*

I will.

Anna looked up from the iPad and at her own reflection. She was wearing green surgical attire, the same uniform the doctors at the hospital used when operating on a patient. She had stolen that and a mask, along with the equipment she had in her briefcase from the hospital where she worked as a nurse. She opened the briefcase and looked at the various scalpels, the syringe filled with the sedative drug. This time she had chosen a drug that would leave the patient sedated, but still conscious. She wanted him to see everything, but not be able to move. As a nurse anesthetist, she knew everything there was to know about sedative drugs and which ones to use. It was also very easy to get a hold of them.

Almost too easy.

Anna listened to the voices behind the wall, waiting for them to be done with the sexual act. It was always the same. They would have sex and then the woman would leave. They never spent the night. It was perfect.

Cheating bastards.

Listening to Michael's voice through the wall only made her anger rise. Oh how she loathed this man. More than anything in this world, she hated everything about him. But that only made her revenge that much sweeter, didn't it?

Anna closed the briefcase as she heard the door to the room next door close. She looked at herself one last time.

Showtime.

She walked out into the hallway, then found the dry erase marker and pushed it into the bottom of the lock with a little smile, thinking of Valdemar. Destiny's cruel irony had laughed at her once, now she was the one laughing back. It was kind of ironic that it was Valdemar's invention that now helped her avenge his death.

She walked inside and found Michael sleeping in the bed. He was snoring slightly and she watched him for a few seconds, before she found the injection needle and emptied it into his arm. The poke to his skin woke him up. Michael gasped and stared at her. At first scared and confused, then relaxed.

"Anna?" he asked.

She nodded, then pulled the mask down so he could see

her better. She wanted him to see her, to face her and realize what he had done and what she was now going to do to him.

"What are you doing here?" He asked when he realized where he was. "Why are you here?" He tried to sit up in the bed, but his arms refused to cooperate. "What is this?" He said and saw the syringe in Anna's hand. "What have you done to me?"

"I have sedated you Michael. Now you can't move."

"But ... but ..." If he was trying to get up again, Anna could no longer see it. She imagined he was and the frustration going through his mind right now. And she enjoyed it.

"What do you want from me? Why have you done this to me?"

Anna tilted her head and smiled. "I'm taking your heart, Michael. It's okay. You never used it anyway."

55

AUGUST 2012

PETER DRAGGED ME UP the stairs. I followed unwillingly, but for the sake of my daughter, I thought I'd better obey. Besides, Peter was right. There was no way we would be able to get out of here in this storm. And there was no way anyone would come here. Not even Mrs. Holm. We were stuck. Isolated. And worst of all, my dad was in the hospital and I had no idea how he was doing, whether he was going to survive or not.

"Peter, why are you doing this to us?" I asked.

He slapped me once again across the face with a grin. "Because I can."

Then he dragged me up another set of stairs. "Where are you taking me? I don't want to get up there."

"Go."

I did as he said and climbed up the small set of stairs that seemed to get narrower and narrower the higher we got. "What's up here, Peter?"

"My studio," he said and pushed me through an old wooden door.

"What about Julie? She might be scared."

"Julie is fine. She's staying in her room. Now go," he said and pushed me inside a huge room under the roof. It was light and very open. If it wasn't for what met me there, I would have thought it was a nice place to be. I got up and looked around, feeling like I was in some sort of torture chamber. The walls were plastered with pictures of people in pain. Dead bodies swimming in tanks with some strange liquid, body parts everywhere and organs in jars.

"What's all this?" I asked.

"Isn't it glorious? It's my exhibition," Peter said.

"What do you mean, exhibition? What is all this?"

"They are all masterpieces. Contributions from killers all over the country. They send me either their first kill or parts of it or some other sort of contribution. I, in return, help them kill and not get caught. I'm sort of a consultant. Soon all of this is going to be an exhibition. Won't be open to the public naturally, only for the inaugurated. And the ticket prices are, naturally, going to be sky high. I think killers from all over the world would want to come here and see this, don't you? It might even give them new ideas. Be inspirational."

I stared at Peter completely freaked out. What kind of a monster was he?

"Look at this one," he said and pointed. "He's new. I haven't prepared him properly yet."

I looked at the sign underneath the body in an open body bag. "Martin Damsgaard," I read out loud. I looked at Peter. "That's the guy who had his liver removed and died from it. You stole his body? Why Peter?"

"It was given to me by the one who killed him. I helped him to be a killer and he contributed with his first kill. He will bring in another contribution later this week. You see, all the organs he stole from people weren't being sold on the black market. No, he lost his son last year and has the remains of the body in his freezer at home. He's replacing the boy's internal organs one by one and placing new, fresh ones in. The body was in the ground for almost a year when he dug him out and took him home. So, naturally, a lot had decomposed by then. Now he is building him again and, soon, he will deliver him to me. It's going to look great here, don't you think?"

"I ... I have no idea what to think, Peter."

"Oh, you have got to see this one as well. You're going to love this." Peter grabbed my arm and dragged me through what he referred to as his exhibition. I felt nauseated and fought the urge to throw up. Peter stopped in front of a body that had been stabbed to death with what looked like five knives going through his chest. I thought I had seen this somewhere before, but couldn't recall where.

"This is the Michael Oestergaard exhibition," Peter said. "You remember him, don't you?"

"The what?"

"Michael Oestergaard. You know the guy who killed using the glove from the Freddy Krueger movies? Remember him? Most unfortunate that you had to have him put away. This was his first kill using the glove. Just to try it out and get past that first kill with it. The guy meant nothing to him. It was random. Just to know how the glove worked, you know. I helped him with all of his kills. I came up with the idea of using the glove from back then. Neat right?"

"You know Michael Oestergaard?"

"We went to the same boarding school. You know, Herlufsholm?"

"Oh my god. You've been ... I can't believe it ... you've

been ... have you been behind this, behind him and others? Pulling the strings like they were puppets?"

"Well, that is giving me way too much credit, dearie, but yes, they come to me for advice and I give it to them. I am, after all, a true expert in killing."

"I had no idea you were that insane. Peter, this is so sick."

"Oh thank you. You're flattering me. This one over here, I believe you know that one as well."

"'The Christian Lonstedt contribution," I said.

"His first too."

"Let me guess the next belongs to Bjarne Larsen from Arnakke?"

"I'm afraid that one worked on his own. Him and that kid of his. Genius with the polonium, though. Couldn't have come up with it better myself. I only wish I had some of his here. But can't have them all, can we?"

"I guess not," I said and looked in direction of the door. Peter had shut it, but I didn't know if it was locked. I had to find a way out and get Julie out with me. Until then, I had to just please Peter and pretend I wasn't frightened to death.

"But I do have one from Allan Witt. Several as a matter of fact, but I only kept the one. He had a tendency to eat his victims and send the remains to me. I did, however, really badly want the princess, but he never gave me that. So I killed him. He was worthless in the end anyway. Went completely insane," Peter said and chuckled.

"Oh my God, the chat room," I said. "You're Thomas De Quincey, aren't you? You ordered me killed, didn't you?"

Peter shrugged with a smile. "Guilty as charged. Nice name, don't you think? He wrote the essay *On Murder Considered as One of the Fine Arts* in 1827. He wrote about the *Society for the Encouragement of Murder* and that's how I got my idea. De Quincey wrote that the members of this secret gentlemen's club *profess to be curious in homicide, amateurs and dilettanti in the various modes of carnage, and, in short, Murder-Fanciers. Every fresh atrocity of that class which the police annals of Europe bring up, they meet and criticize as they would a picture, statue, or other work of art."*

"But Peter, his essay was satirical. It's fiction. It's a joke."

"I know that," Peter said. "But he gave me the idea. Once I was back from Iraq, I missed the action, I missed the war, so I kept going back either to Iraq or Afghanistan, but I was never quite satisfied. It just wasn't as fun when it was war, you know. I needed something new, so that's how I came up with my own club for killer artists like me."

"Artists? What the hell are you talking about?"

"The art of killing of course." Peter paused and looked around. "Do try and keep up here, Rebekka. I hate having to repeat things."

I remained shocked and speechless.

"Oh, you need to see this as well," he said with pride. "This is what I think will make people want to come from all over the world."

Peter grabbed my arm and dragged me again. I followed him fearing what would come next.

"'This one is quite impressive," he said. "Look at all the gold on the caskets."

"Is that the remains of the two kings? You are the one who stole the dead kings from the churches?"

"Yes. They're perfect for my purpose. You see both of them were murdered. The murder of Erik Klipping is still unsolved to this day. Fits right into my exhibition, I figured."

I shook my head, not understanding how I had not seen how insane Peter really had become. He had fooled us all, hadn't he? Pretending to have changed when, in fact, it was much worse than any nightmare I could have imagined.

"Oh and the last part. The best part, well, for me at least, since it's my contribution," Peter said and dragged me again.

"It's empty Peter. There is nothing there," I said and stared at the vacant wall.

"Yes, but imagine the entire wall plastered with photos of someone who knows they are about to die, and then slowly dying ... documented with a picture each minute of their dying hours. Wouldn't that be neat? I don't think the world has ever seen that before. Read the sign."

I looked at the wall again and found the small metal plate. My heart stopped as I read it.

Rebekka Franck's dying minutes.

56

AUGUST 2012

"WHAT THE HELL IS this Anna? What are you going to do? What do you mean you'll take my heart?"

Anna looked at the man she had once loved and smiled. "I meant just what I said, Michael. See, I have been collecting new organs for our son, and all I need is a new heart."

"But ... but Valdemar is dead?" I don't understand."

"I dug him up. I wanted to be with him. Do you have any idea how much I miss him every day of my life, do you Michael?"

"N ... No."

"Where were you, Michael?" Anna asked.

"Where was I ... when? Anna, I really don't think you're well ..."

Anna leaned in over Michael's numb body. He was still naked. She looked into his eyes and shook her head slowly. "Where were you when he died, Michael?"

"I ... I don't know. How am I supposed to know?" Michael said with a shivering voice.

"How are you supposed to know? Well, any normal

father who cared would know exactly where he was at the moment his son died. I know where I was, Michael. I was right next to him. I had given him a part of my one lung, but it wasn't enough. I begged the doctor to take more, to take whatever my son needed, but he refused. It would kill me, he said and he wasn't allowed to do that. Can you imagine, Michael sitting there holding him in your arms while he draws his last breath? Huh? Can you? No, of course you can't, 'cause you WEREN'T there, were you? Did you look into his big beautiful eyes and tell him how sorry you were that you couldn't save him, did you? No you didn't. But I did, Michael. I held him with these arms, these two arms while he slowly died. And then I screamed, Michael. I screamed and cried in anger because, if anyone deserved to live, it was him. Because I knew he could have lived, if only his dad hadn't been such a BASTARD."

Anna was crying now and lifted the scalpel into the light to make sure Michael saw it. His eyes grew wide. "Anna, I ... I ..."

"It's too late, Michael. There is nothing you can say to bring him back to me. He was my everything, Michael. He was all I had and now ... now I'm alone. Alone with my shame, alone with my guilt that I couldn't save my only son. Where were you, Michael? Were you with your new family? With your new son?"

"I ... I don't kno ..."

"Of course you don't. Because you don't care, do you? And then, what happens next? I call his dad's office to let him know that his son died and when the funeral is." Anna fought her tears and anger. She spoke through gritted teeth. "You didn't even show up for the funeral, Michael. You just had your secretary send a flower arrangement."

"I was out of town."

"Doing what, Michael? Selling your new product? Selling the new game that saved your company and saved your job, huh? And tell me, Michael, what is the name of that game, huh? The game you're now making millions off of? The game you pretend is yours?"

A shadow crossed Michael's face.

"What's the name of it, Michael?" Anna yelled.

"Mindskill," Michael said with a low voice.

"Mindskill, huh? Now, is that a coincidence? Your son created a game with the exact same name. It couldn't, by any chance, be the same game, now could it? NO you would never just steal it, would you? You would at least give him the credit and maybe send a check to his mother every now and then since it has become such a huge success, am I right? How could you, Michael? You know that all he ever wanted was for you to accept him, for you to see how smart he was and for you to love him despite his handicap. Why couldn't you just do that? Everything he ever did, he did to make you proud, to make you finally see him. You couldn't even give him the credit for having invented the game could you?"

"Look Anna, if this is about the money, then I am willing to ..."

"It was never about any money. I don't need your blood money. Valdemar doesn't need your blood money. We don't need anything from you. We don't want anything from you." Anna paused and looked at Michael's chest. "Except for your heart."

Then she lifted the scalpel and sank it into his skin. Michael screamed as he watched Anna make an eight-inch incision cut down the center of his chest wall. Then, she cut his breastbone and opened his rib cage to reach his heart, when suddenly, someone knocked on the door.

"We don't want to be disturbed," she yelled, but the knocking didn't stop.

"Room service," the person outside yelled. Anna took off her gloves, walked to the door, and opened it just enough to peek out. "We didn't order any ..." Then she paused. The face greeting her on the other side of the door was suddenly very familiar.

"So Bill Durgin is a woman, huh?" The man said. "Well I'll be damned."

57

AUGUST 2012

"**PETER, PLEASE, DON'T DO** this to me." Peter had put me in a straitjacket and was now tightening it on my back so I couldn't move. Then, he tied me to a plank of some sort.

"You know, I found this among a bunch of equipment in the basement recently. I believe it must have been used back when the place was a mental hospital. It's exciting to think about who might have worn it before, don't you think? It could have been a famous historical person."

"I doubt it, Peter."

Peter laughed. "Well, maybe not. But I do have a feeling about this place. You know, back when you first left me, I came out here and often spent weeks here, just walking the hallways and discovering the place. I have made many friends here. The place is filled with history. Like that doctor that I told you about. I have met him. He killed himself after killing more than a hundred patients here doing all kinds of experiments on them. He shot himself and his family in room 237, but every now and then, I meet him in there. He has a big hole in his head from the shot right here, and there is blood all over the walls and floor," Peter said and put a finger to his forehead with a grin.

"Peter, you're hurting me. It's too tight," I said. "Please just let me go, will you? Let me and Julie go. You don't want to hurt us, I know you Peter."

Peter lifted his camera and took a series of pictures. "There you go. The first one for the wall. The one where you start pleading for your life." He giggled in delight. "Isn't this fun? Oh, did you know that back when this place was a hospital for the mentally ill, they simply called the patients 'lunatics'? It's the truth; that's what the doctor told me. Back then, the mentally ill were people who had to be put away, they were an embarrassment to the family, so they were often forgotten once they arrived here at the asylum. So, the dear doctor could perform any experiment and treatment he pleased. No one ever cared."

I stared at Peter, wondering how I was ever going to get out of this. Julie was still downstairs and I just hoped that she would stay safe. "That's all very interesting, Peter, but what are you going to do to me?" I asked, thinking it would be best if I kept the conversation going. Maybe an opening would come. Maybe I could talk him out of it.

"Oh, I have something extraordinary planned for you, Rebekka, dearie. Don't you worry about that. It's going to be spectacular."

Peter walked towards a small box covered by a cloth. Peter looked at me with excitement in his eyes and pulled the cloth off.

"Ta-da."

A small cage appeared underneath. Inside of it was a huge rat. He was staring at me with empty black eyes and vibrating whiskers. I had always hated rats more than anything in this world. Any nightmare I'd ever had, always contained at least one rat. Peter knew that.

"Peter. You know I hate rats. What are you doing with that?" I said, with my heart in my throat.

Peter opened the cage, took out the rat, and held it in his hand. I started breathing heavier, gasping in fear of what he was going to do with it.

"Isn't he a beauty?" Peter said and lifted the rat so I could better look at it. "It was actually the doctor who came up with the idea. He told me that he used rats in many of his experiments. See, back in the late eighteen hundreds, when this place was an asylum, the doctor thought rats were able to find diseases in the human body and eat them. One of his many theories was that mental illness was caused by something growing inside of the patient, overshadowing the patient's way of thinking, making them think they saw things they didn't and making them filled with fear and so on. So, his theory was that the rats would be able to detect the disease in the body and remove it like trash from a garbage can."

"So, what did he do?" I asked with a shivering voice.

"You'll see," Peter said. "It's very simple really." Peter grinned and found a metal bucket. Then he placed the bucket on top of my stomach and put the rat underneath it.

I felt sick to my stomach just thinking of the creature on top of me. Peter then found an old Bunsen burner that reminded me of chemistry lab in high school.

"Peter what are you doing?"

Peter found his camera and took another series of pictures before he turned on the Bunsen burner, then started heating up the metal bucket. "Peter I don't like this," I cried. "What are you doing?"

"As the container is being gradually heated, the rat will

begin to look for a way out. The only way out is through the patient's body. Digging a hole, by gnawing its way through the straitjacket and then your skin, will probably take a few hours of agonizing pain for you. And then result in certain death."

58

AUGUST 2012

IT DIDN'T TAKE LONG before I started feeling the rat gnawing on the straitjacket. The thought of those teeth soon nibbling my skin scared me to death. My entire body was shivering in fear.

"Peter I promise I'll ... I'll do anything for you."

Peter stroked my head gently. "Oh, but dear Rebekka. You just aren't well, are you? You need to be cleansed. The doctor told me how I could cure you."

"But Peter," I cried. "This will kill me. You told me so yourself."

"But then you'll be made immortal afterwards, Rebekka. Through my pictures, through my art, you'll stay alive for eternity."

Slowly I felt the straitjacket gave in to the rat's sharp teeth. "Peter please, don't do this ..."

As I spoke, suddenly a sound interrupted me. Peter heard it too and turned to look. I couldn't believe my eyes. In through the door came Henrik Fenger. He looked like he had been through hell and back. His clothes and hair were soaking wet, his eyes looked like those of a mad man.

"Who the hell are you?" Peter asked. "What are you doing here? This is private property."

I wanted to scream for help, but somehow the expression on Henrik Fenger's face made me hesitate. I was whimpering while feeling the rat gnawing through the jacket and now reaching the fabric of my shirt. Next would be my bare skin.

"Thomas De Quincey, I presume?" Henrik Fenger said.

Peter growled and walked closer. "Who the hell are you? Who told you where to find me?"

"Anna," Henrik Fenger said. "You probably know her as Bill Durgin. I killed her a couple of hours ago. You told her to bring you her contribution, remember? She told me all about it before I slit her throat with her own scalpel. You were stupid enough to give her this address where she was supposed to bring the body of her son. Quite the wacko, huh? Trying to keep her dead son alive by putting in new organs? What a lunatic."

Henrik Fenger had developed a tic in his left eye and was constantly blinking now. I could feel the rat's teeth on the other side of the fabric.

"I don't know what you're talking about. We're kind of in the middle of something here," Peter said. He had clenched his fist and was waiting for the right moment to attack Henrik Fenger. Henrik saw it too, but he didn't seem the least bit scared. More like he was really angry.

"She was a loose end anyway, Thomas," Henrik said. "It was too easy to figure out where she was. She wrote, or rather Billy wrote that she was watching her next victim eating soft tofu soup. Well anyone travelling in hotels in Denmark knows there is only one hotel that serves only vegan, organic food and that's Skal's Hotel in Vensyssel. See the thing is, everybody knows it, but it's the only hotel in

Vendsyssel and there isn't a restaurant anywhere near, so you're kind of stuck with their annoying food, aren't you? So I figured that no man, and we knew all of her victims were travelling men, didn't we? Well cheating travelling men, that is. So, I figured that no man would want to eat tofu soup unless he was forced to, if you know what I mean."

"I really don't care," Peter said. He lifted his clenched fist and stormed against Henrik. He punched him and cracked his lip, but to my surprise Henrik didn't even move. Blood was running down his chin and he still didn't even stop smiling.

"Is that it, Thomas? Is that all you've got? 'Cause I've gotta say, it wasn't much of a punch." Henrik lifted his clenched fist and slammed it into Peter's face. The blow forced him to stumble backwards. I gasped while watching Peter's eyes roll back in his head. His nose bled heavily. He landed on the floor and his head was still spinning when he sat up.

"Now try again, Thomas 'cause I really was looking forward to a proper fight. After all, you were the guy who gave Anna the idea that she should take my kidney, now weren't you? You are the guy I have been searching for. The mastermind, or should I say kingpin? Maybe you just need a little more motivation. Maybe if I told you I killed Karl Persson as well. And ... uh ... Michael Cogliantry and Alex Andreyer. Everyone in that pathetic little chat room of yours. I pretended to be Karl and then set up a meeting with each and every one of them. Told them we should go on a killing spree together. Guess it wasn't a complete lie, huh?" Henrik laughed.

Peter finally managed to get to his feet, then stormed towards Henrik, slamming his fist into his face, causing Henrik to fall backwards. Then Peter was all over him. I tried to move in my straitjacket and suddenly realized that the rat had bitten its way through what was holding my arms. Suddenly my arms were loosened and I was able to move them. My right hand was soon freed and I managed to hit the bucket onto the ground. I screamed as I saw the rat. It was still gnawing on my clothes, but as soon as it realized the bucket was gone, it shrieked and jumped for the ground. I twisted my body back and forth and soon, my other hand was free as well, and I was able to squirm out of the jacket. Panting, I put my feet on the ground and watched as the two men fought each other, panting, throwing punches, yelling and groaning.

I looked around me to see if I could spot a second exit and found a small door in the other end of the room, behind a part of Peter's macabre exhibition. I opened it and snuck through. I ran down the stairs, stormed into Julie's room, and found her on the bed. She had been crying. In her hand she was holding my cellphone that Peter had taken from me and left in the kitchen when he dragged me upstairs.

"I called the police," she said. "They should be here any minute."

EPILOGUE

I was holding my dad's hand when he woke up. Three days had passed since I had escaped the castle in Brabrand holding Julie in my arms. While we were running outside, we heard sirens blaring in the distance. We found the boat Henrik had used to get to the island and sailed away to safety while hundreds of officers stormed the house.

Apparently, Peter had put up a fight, so the officers had ended up shooting him, while Henrik Fenger was arrested for breaking and entering. He ended up paying a fine. The police never could find evidence enough to accuse him of any of the killings that I knew he had committed. The story had gone worldwide about the lunatic man alone in a castle on an isolated island who wanted to make the exhibition from hell. The kings' coffins were returned to the churches and I took Julie back to Karrebaeksminde to be with my dad while he was recovering.

"Sweetie," he mumbled and opened his eyes. "I'm so glad to see you."

"You're doing much better, Dad. Don't worry. The doctor says I can take you home, maybe tomorrow."

My dad chuckled. "No, that's not what I meant. I'm glad you're here because someone came in earlier. I told him to come later today so he could see you."

"Hi Rebekka."

I turned my head and looked into the eyes of Sune. I rose to my feet and let go of my dad's hand. "Sune? What are you doing here? Jens-Ole said you quit. I thought you had left town."

Sune smiled. "I was about to, but I wanted to say goodbye to your dad. He has, after all, meant a lot to me. He convinced me I should at least say a proper goodbye to you."

My heart was pounding in my chest. There was so much I wanted to say, but why? To make him stay? Was that what I wanted? Him to stay against his will just because I might or might not be pregnant with his child? I had my doubts.

"Did you hear about ...?"

Sune nodded. "Peter? Yeah. I heard. Quite the story, huh?"

I exhaled. "The funeral is Friday. I guess we'll be there, since Julie needs to say goodbye to her dad."

"Naturally." Sune looked at me and sighed. "Well okay. I'd better ... I should just ... I mean we need to be in Copenhagen at three, so I should ..."

"Stop." I looked at Sune. It had burst out without me even thinking. Our eyes locked. I gasped. My tongue felt so dry. I could hardly move my lips.

"Argh, for Christ sake," my dad grumbled. "She's pregnant and the child is probably yours."

My heart stopped. I wanted to yell at my dad for blurting it out like that. But then I saw the look on Sune's face.

"Is it true?" Sune asked.

"Well ... uh ... I guess it is. Yes, Sune, yes. I'm pregnant."

Sune's eyes grew wide. He was breathing heavily.

"You don't have to do anything, Sune. It's okay. After all it might be Peter's."

"But it might be mine?"

"Well, yes. I mean we did try for a long time ... and the dates fit. The doctor told me it happened by the end of June and there was no Peter then. Not until July."

Sune smiled widely. "I'm gonna be a dad again? We're going to be parents?"

"I guess so?"

Sune grabbed me around my waist and picked me up. He started spinning around with me in his arms. I laughed. He stopped and let me slide down slightly till my eyes were in front of his.

"I love you Rebekka Franck."

"I love you too."

Then we kissed.

THE END

DO you wanna know what happens next?

Get *ELEVEN, TWELVE ... DIG AND DELVE*.

Dear reader,

Thank you for purchasing *Nine, Ten ... Never sleep again..* I hope you have enjoyed the crazy journey so far. Don't forget to get the next in the series. It is my plan to write many more stories about Rebekka and Sune in the future.

If you enjoyed this series then you might also enjoy my Emma Frost-series. I have included an excerpt from *Slenderman* (Emma Frost Book 9) on the following pages. Get the entire series by following the links below.

Don't forget to check out my other books as well. You can buy them by following the links below. And don't forget to leave reviews if possible. It means so much to me to hear what you think.

Take care,
Willow Rose

Connect with Willow online and you will be the first to know about new releases and bargains from Willow Rose.

Sign up to the* VIP *email here:
http://eepurl.com/vVfEf
I promise not to share your email with anyone else, and I won't clutter your inbox. I'll only contact you when a new book is out or when I have a special bargain/free eBook.

Follow Willow Rose on BookBub:
https://www.bookbub.com/authors/willow-rose

MYSTERY/HORROR NOVELS

- In One Fell Swoop
- Umbrella Man
- Blackbird Fly
- To Hell in a Handbasket
- Edwina

7TH STREET CREW SERIES

- What Hurts the Most
- You Can Run
- You Can't Hide
- Careful Little Eyes

EMMA FROST SERIES

- Itsy Bitsy Spider
- Miss Dolly had a Dolly
- Run, Run as Fast as You Can
- Cross Your Heart and Hope to Die
- Peek-a-Boo I See You
- Tweedledum and Tweedledee
- Easy as One, Two, Three
- There's No Place like Home
- Slenderman
- Where the Wild Roses Grow

JACK RYDER SERIES

- Hit the Road Jack
- Slip out the Back Jack
- The House that Jack Built
- Black Jack

REBEKKA FRANCK SERIES

- One, Two...He is Coming for You
- Three, Four...Better Lock Your Door
- Five, Six...Grab your Crucifix
- Seven, Eight...Gonna Stay up Late
- Nine, Ten...Never Sleep Again
- Eleven, Twelve...Dig and Delve
- Thirteen, Fourteen...Little Boy Unseen

HORROR SHORT-STORIES

- Better watch out
- Eenie, Meenie
- Rock-a-Bye Baby
- Nibble, Nibble, Crunch
- Humpty Dumpty
- Chain Letter
- Mommy Dearest
- The Bird

PARANORMAL SUSPENSE/FANTASY NOVELS

AFTERLIFE SERIES

- Beyond
- Serenity
- Endurance
- Courageous

THE WOLFBOY CHRONICLES

- A Gypsy Song
- I am WOLF

DAUGHTERS OF THE JAGUAR

- Savage
- Broken

ABOUT THE AUTHOR

The Queen of Scream, Willow Rose, is an international best-selling author. She writes Mystery/Suspense/Horror, Paranormal Romance and Fantasy. She is inspired by authors like James Patterson, Agatha Christie, Stephen King, Anne Rice, and Isabel Allende. She lives on Florida's Space Coast with her husband and two daughters. When she is not writing or reading, you'll find her surfing and watching the dolphins play in the waves of the Atlantic Ocean. She has sold more than two million books.

Connect with Willow online:

willow-rose.net
madamewillowrose@gmail.com

SLENDERMAN

EXCERPT

For a special sneak peak of Willow Rose's Bestselling Mystery Novel **Slenderman** turn to the next page.

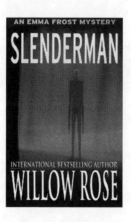

Someone's always watching me
Someone's always there
When I'm sleeping he just waits,
and he stares

Someone's always standing in
the darkest corner of my room
He's tall and wears a suit in black,
dressed like the perfect groom

Where are you going?
Why won't you stay?
They might be scared of you,
but I just want to play

He has no face
He hides with the trees
He loves little children when they beg and scream...
Please!

Slendy's Lullaby by LilyPichu
https://www.youtube.com/Slendy's Lullaby

PROLOGUE

NOVEMBER 2014

SOMEONE WAS WATCHING HIM. Rasmus Krohn was happy to finally see his friend again. He turned his head and glared at the door to his bedroom, to make sure no one was awake in the house other than him. It was one in the morning. They should all be asleep.

Rasmus turned his head to face the screen again. With much eagerness, he let his fingers dance across the keyboard.

>Hi there. Where have you been?<

>Hello<

Rasmus thought he heard a sound, and turned to look at the door once again. He held his breath. Someone was in the hallway outside. He followed the steps as they walked across the carpet. It sounded like his father. The steps were heavy, not like his mother's that were usually light because she would be tiptoeing in order to not wake up the kids. Rasmus followed the sound of the steps and breathed in relief when they passed his door and continued towards the bathroom. There was a bump, then his father complaining and cursing. After that, the door was closed. Rasmus breathed again. He turned off the small lamp on his desk next to the computer. The light coming from under his door could reveal him.

He received a new message from his friend.

>Are you ready?<

Rasmus looked at the blinking message on the bottom of the screen. He heard his dad flush the toilet and the water start running. The old man cursed again, probably bumped his toe or his head, as usual, the drunk. Rasmus held his breath as his dad opened the door to the bathroom and entered the hallway again. He turned down the light on the screen to low and sat in darkness. Rasmus's dad walked across the carpet outside, then stopped. Rasmus's heart was pounding in his chest. He could sense his dad was right outside his door now.

Would he come in to check on him? Or to pull him out of bed and start beating on him like last time?

His parents had told Rasmus so many times not to use his computer at night. Especially on a school night. His dad would be furious if he found out.

The seconds that passed felt like years. Everything inside of him was screaming. If his father walked through that door and found him by the computer, it was all over. They would take the computer away, they had told him... even though Rasmus had saved up for it and paid for it on his own. It wasn't good for him, his mother said.

As if she has any idea what's good for me! She doesn't even know how to take care of herself, let alone her children.

Rasmus stared at the bed and wondered if he could make it over there if the door handle moved. He could sense his dad was out there still. He even believed he could smell the booze on his breath.

Just go to bed, you fucking drunk. Leave me alone. Leave all of us alone!

Rasmus's hands were shaking when he remembered what had happened the last time his father had come through that door at night. He still had the bruise on his back from the baseball bat.

Just go back to bed, you asshole! Find someone else to bother.

He felt the rage rising inside of him. The humiliation was the worst; the fact that he still couldn't fight back was painful. At the age of fifteen, Rasmus was still scrawny. No one took him seriously. No one regarded him as anyone. But soon, they would. He was going to make sure of that.

The steps moved on across the carpet and Rasmus breathed again. He heard the door to his parents' bedroom shut and everything go quiet again. He closed his eyes and leaned back in the chair for a few seconds before he turned up the light on the screen again. The expressionless white face of the tall and slender man stared back at him from behind the screen. He had written a new message.

>It's time<

1

NOVEMBER 2014

I HAD TIPTOED around the cigar box for two weeks now. I was back in my house after the renovation which followed the fire, and sitting in my wonderful new kitchen with a coffee and a pastry, staring at the box on the table in front of me.

I hadn't opened it yet.

The construction workers gave it to me after we were allowed to move back in. One of the men handed it to me, telling me he had no idea what else to do with it.

"We found it when we fixed the roof. It fell out when we removed the old wood and replaced it with the new," he said.

The man in the yellow helmet followed his statement with a shrug, and I took the old dirty box out of his hands. It had been with me ever since. I had taken it in my purse with me everywhere, and taken it out now and then to look at it, but never opened it. Not yet, at least.

"Aren't you curious?" Morten had asked several times when he caught me staring at it. "Why don't you take a look?"

"I'm extremely curious," I answered.

Yet, I still hadn't dared to open it. It wasn't like me at all. What was I afraid of? I asked myself over and over. I didn't know. I kind of felt like the box didn't belong to me. Like I was intruding somehow on someone's personal life. Like I was supposed to find its original owners and give it back. But I had no idea who they were. I didn't even know if anyone would care enough about it to want it back. It wasn't an ordinary box. Anyone could tell it wasn't. It was dusty and dirty from being up there under the roof behind the wood. Someone had cared enough about it to hide it well for many years. Maybe it was of importance to that person. Maybe I was violating this person's need to keep whatever was in it hidden?

The thought only made me more curious.

I touched the front again and ran my hand across it. On the cover was a handwritten name in cursive.

Larsen

"Maybe it belonged to your grandmother?" Morten had asked, but it wasn't my family's name. It wasn't even my grandmother's maiden name. I didn't know any Larsen. It was a pretty common name here in Denmark, so it could be anyone.

I tapped my fingers on the kitchen table and sipped my coffee. I had decided that today would be the day when I finally opened the lid. My fingers marched across the top.

Just a little peek won't hurt anyone.

I tried telling myself that maybe by opening it I could figure out to whom it belonged and maybe get it back to the rightful owners. It just seemed so private. My fingers touched the front once again and stroked it gently, while I wondered what great things could be in there. I kind of enjoyed having my own little fantasy about what it would reveal, and some part of me was really afraid to be disappointed as well. Maybe that was why I hadn't opened it yet. Maybe I was simply afraid of ruining the illusion. I was afraid of finding cooking recipes or grocery lists or something boring. I wanted this to be special. That was also why I waited till the house was empty before I finally lifted the lid with the tips of my fingers. I held my breath as I finally pulled it off. I was about to close it again, thinking I had no right to be going through it, but curiosity won. After all, it could just be cooking recipes, and then no one would feel like I had invaded their private life. Maybe there were even some I could use?

Slowly, I looked inside. My heart was pounding in my chest as I pulled out a stack of letters, all neatly bound together with a ribbon. I put the letters on the table and took in a deep breath. Carefully, I untied the ribbon. All the letters were addressed to the same person, my grandmother. I opened one and started reading the contents. Two pages fully written from top to bottom in cursive using blue ink. A date was at the top.

March 22nd 1959.

I read the first sentence out loud to myself.

"Dearest sister. He is the most beautiful child in the world."

2

MARCH 1959

HE IS THE MOST beautiful child in the world. I can't believe how lucky I am. Oh, sister. I wish you were here with me. You'd be as enchanted as I am.

Helle Larsen glanced at her baby, who was sleeping in the crib next to her desk at the nursery where she was writing her letter. She couldn't believe how good he had been. Only three weeks old, and already sleeping through the night. He was nothing like his brothers. They had kept her up all night for weeks until she finally let them cry through the night. It wasn't something she had enjoyed; as a matter of fact, it was the worst part about having a baby. To have to ignore them night after night till they finally gave up. If it had been Helle's choice, she would have kept going in to the nursery to take care of them to make sure they didn't feel left alone, but both the nurse and her mother had told her this was the way to do it. This was the way they had done it for years. It was best for her, they said. That way, she would get her rest, and the children would know who was in charge.

"After a few weeks, they'll figure it out," Helle's mother

had said. "If you keep going in there every night, they'll keep crying. It's very simple. If you don't come, they give up."

So, now that Per already slept through the night, and had done so for almost a week, Helle hoped she wouldn't have to go through the same process as with the two others. Hopefully, it wouldn't be necessary.

"Helle!"

Her husband was calling from downstairs. Helle finished the letter, put it in an envelope and put her sister's name and address on it before she hurried out of the nursery, careful not to wake up her sleeping son. She rushed down the stairs. Her husband Claes was standing in the kitchen with his muddy boots planted on her newly washed floors.

"Where's my lunch?" he yelled.

"It's in the refrigerator, ready for you," she said, and ran to the refrigerator and pulled out a plate with four slices of rye bread with four different toppings. One with herring and onions, one with liver pate, one with mackerel, and one with cheese.

Claes growled and took the plate out of her hand.

"I didn't know when you were coming in," she argued, to excuse herself for his lunch not being on the table. Her husband was with the animals all day, or in the fields of their farm, and only had a short time to eat. And it was never at the same time that he decided it was time to eat. He was always busy and always grumpy.

Helle never took much notice of his moods, especially not since she had the baby. Nothing in the world could make her unhappy these days. Not even Claes' growling or complaining.

"What, no egg today? What about pork roast? You know how much I love the pork roast."

"I thought you'd like something else today, so I gave you mackerel instead," she said, listening carefully in case Per woke up. She missed him so much when he was sleeping. "The doctor told me fish is so good for you."

Claes grumbled while he ate. It had been a long time since Helle had lost any interest she might have had in the man, and now she felt less than ever for him. But, he provided well for the family, and with that she was content. He worked hard on their farm and gave her a life where she could take care of her three sons without having to work much, other than help him out here and there with the feeding of the pigs and such. Helle poured Claes a schnapps to go with the herring. It stopped the growling.

"Where are Ulrik and Peter?" she asked. The two older boys always helped out around the farm on weekends when they didn't have school. Helle had prepared lunches for them as well, and put them in the fridge.

The mention of their names made the growling come back. Claes chewed loudly, smacking his mouth, sounding much like the pigs in the pen. He'd even started to look like one over the years, she thought to herself with a grin.

"I told them to run their bikes down to old Hansen and ask him if he needs any help."

Claes growled and ate some more. Helle regained some of her affection for the man and remembered why she had liked him when they got married. He was very generous beneath that grumpy exterior. He could be so considerate. Old Hansen had recently slipped and hurt his hip, and he had no sons to take over the farm after him, or to take care of him when he needed it. Claes desperately needed the boys' help around his own farm, so it was a huge gesture on his part.

"That was nice of you," she said. "They'll eat when they get back."

Just as she had said those last words, she heard Per cry from upstairs and rushed up to get him, while smiling at the prospect of being able to spend time with her baby again.

3

NOVEMBER 2014

ULRIK LARSEN WAS SITTING on his couch waiting for the nurse to arrive. He glared at the picture next to the TV. Elsebeth was smiling back at him from behind the glass.

"What are you smiling at?" he growled.

She had left him a year ago and, ever since, life hadn't been much worth living. Still, he had to do it. He had to finish the race. Even if it meant becoming as helpless as a baby again. Life had a way with irony, hadn't it? Here he was at the end of his life, and he couldn't even go to the bathroom alone. They had given him a diaper. He peed through a hole in the side into a small plastic bag that they changed every morning and evening.

At least they hadn't put him in a home yet. He was grateful for that. It was part of a new politic, his daughter had explained to him. They wanted the elderly to stay in their homes for as long as possible, so instead they would send a nurse twice a day. In the morning to get him out of bed, remove the diaper and change the bag, then one again in the evening to put him to bed. During the day, he didn't do much except sleep. The city sent someone else over with food on a small tray...enough for three meals during the day. Tasteless colorless food. All he had to do was throw it in the oven or microwave and heat it up. They did everything to make his life as pleasant as possible, they said.

Ulrik would have preferred death.

The only fun he occasionally had was when he grabbed a nurse's behind with a loud laugh, or when he pretended to be senile and tried to kiss them while calling them his wife's name. After a little while, they caught on to him and started sending male nurses instead. That was the end of the fun.

Ulrik coughed and snarled. Where was that nurse? Usually, they arrived around nine p.m., but it was at least fifteen minutes past. They were never on time, but this was too much. Ulrik pulled himself up from the couch and walked across the floor of his old villa that he had shared for thirty years with Elsebeth before she decided to leave him. On the dining table that he never used anymore stood old withered bouquets of flowers and cards lined up telling him happy birthday. It was two months ago that his daughter had surprised him on his sixty-eighth birthday, along with her husband and children. Ulrik never liked surprises much, and he had hated this one in particular. It was his first without Elsebeth, and he didn't feel much like celebrating. When they had arrived in the doorway with balloons and flowers and food in their arms, he told them he wanted them to leave. But, as usual, his daughter didn't listen to her old man.

"Ah, don't be so dull," she had said, and stormed past him, starting to decorate the house while her good-for-nothing husband had started heating the food in the kitchen. Ulrik had tried to make them go away, and even tried growling at the grandchildren, but with no luck. Then, he had turned on the TV and turned up the sound, refusing to leave his favorite place on the couch for as long as the celebration lasted.

He grabbed his walker and walked with it towards the kitchen. He thought of the many nights Elsebeth had prepared coffee for them and always gave him a small butter cookie on the side. Sometimes—especially around Christmas—she would even give him a small piece of marzipan. Oh, how he missed those days. The small gestures of affection that he forgot to thank her for. He hadn't had a cookie or any marzipan since. He didn't even want to celebrate Christmas this year, much to his daughter and grandchildren's surprise.

"But, Dad, you have to come. We'll have fun. You don't have to buy any presents. We'd just like to be with you," his daughter Annie kept telling him.

But he wasn't going. He was waiting for death, and there was nothing to celebrate about that.

Holding on to his walker, Ulrik managed to get himself to the window to look outside to see if he could spot the nurse's car, but the street was empty. Maybe they had forgotten about him? It had happened once before. They had made all kinds of excuses the next day and told him they were very busy and they had many elderly who needed their attention, so he had to cut them some slack. Ulrik had ended up sitting in his own feces all night long on the couch, unable to do anything about it. He hadn't thought it called for him to cut them any slack. But what could he do? Like a baby depended on his mother, so did he depend on their help.

In anger, Ulrik turned to walk back to the couch, fearing that was where he would end up spending the night, since he couldn't get into his bed on his own. As he made the turn, he stared into a white expressionless face.

Finally, death had come for him, he thought, but much to his regret, he didn't feel the satisfaction he had thought he would feel in this moment. It wasn't a feeling of relief that had taken ahold of him. In the seconds the knife sunk into his chest, he was grabbed by a strange fear, and his entire body protested at having to leave now. He let go of the walker and tried to grab out at death standing in front of him. Desperately, he tried to scream, to call for help as he heard the nurse's car drive into the driveway. But he knew it was in vain. It was too late. His time had come. As the tall and slender faceless creature in the black suit in front of him pulled out the knife just to stab it into Ulrik's chest once again, he knew it was too late. Death had finally caught up with him, and it wasn't at all as pleasant as it was cracked up to be.

4

NOVEMBER 2014

I was completely swallowed up by the letters, and kept reading until my children came home from school. The construction workers were still working on my façade and had put a ladder up in front of my kitchen window. I heard Victor throw his bike, then his steps on the stairs and the front door opening. Victor ran to his seat at the kitchen table and sat down.

"Where is my food?"

I put the letters back in the box, and then sprang up. The memories of Helle Larsen's life lingering with me still as I buttered some toasted bread for him and topped it with strawberry jelly. I served the bread, then made some choco-late milk for him.

"So, how was your day?" I asked.

"You asked me that yesterday."

Of course. That was always his answer. I had to try something new. "Did you learn anything new?"

"I never learn anything new," he responded.

I buttered a piece of toasted bread for myself and thought about Helle Larsen preparing afternoon-tea for her family back in '59. Things were really different back then, but a lot remained the same. They had eaten toasted bread with butter and marmalade back then as well.

The door opened again and Maya entered. I smiled. She looked tired. "Rough day, honey?"

She grumbled and threw her backpack on the floor. Things were becoming more and more normal with her lately. Since Dr. Sonnichsen had started working with her, she was gradually improving with every day that passed. She was becoming more and more herself. Even the grumbling and rolling of the eyes was back. I started to regret ever having missed it, but it was a healthy sign, and that made me happy.

"I hate school!" she said, as I placed her toast in front of her. She looked up. "I'm not gonna eat that. How old do you think I am?"

I shrugged and sat down. I took a bite of my own toast. It tasted wonderful.

"It's filled with carbs," she said.

I chuckled. Yup, she was definitely back to normal again. Well, almost. She still had some huge gaps in her memory that I sincerely hoped she would regain. It was frustrating for her from time to time, especially when talking to friends, that she couldn't remember things they had done together. Her short-term memory worked perfectly, but her childhood, and especially the time up until the car-accident, she had almost no recollection of. She remembered her father losing control and hitting both Maya and his new wife. That was why she had run away. But other than that, she remembered nothing. I was unsure if she was ever going to. Dr. Sonnichsen had told me she might block it all out because of how traumatic it had been for her, and that it would come back to her if she ever let it, if she felt like she was ready to deal with it. For some, it never came back.

"You want me to make something else for you?" I asked.

"You have jelly on your teeth, Mom," she snarled. "It looks gross."

I smiled widely to show it to her better. She made a grimace and I laughed.

"That is so disgusting, Mom." Maya got up. "I'm going to my room."

"You're not eating?" I asked, finally licking the jelly off of my teeth. I was worried about Maya. She was hardly eating lately. "I can make you something else. Maybe some yogurt? Or a banana?"

She shook her head. "I'm good. Dr. Sonnichsen is going to be here in an hour, and I want to go on the computer before she gets here."

"So now the computer is more important than eating?" I asked. "What about spending time with your family?"

She scoffed. "What family? You're always with Morten. And my dad? Well, I don't even really know who he is, do I?"

"You have a father. Michael is your father," I argued, but wasn't convincing.

"We both know that isn't true," she said. "I don't even want to see him anymore. There's no reason to."

I couldn't argue against that. He wasn't her real father, and after what he had done to her, I wasn't going to let him into her life anytime soon anyway. Michael was desperately trying to get custody of Victor, even though he hadn't shown much interest in the boy over the last several years. So far, he didn't have much of a case, and I wasn't giving him one.

"Well, you need to eat at some point. You didn't have any breakfast either. Did you eat anything at school at all?"

Maya didn't answer. She grabbed her backpack and stormed out of the kitchen. Seconds later, I heard her slam the door to her room. She had been on the computer a lot lately, and I hadn't decided whether I thought it was a good idea or not. She seemed to be shutting out the world and everyone who loved her.

5

NOVEMBER 2014

HER BAGS WERE HEAVY. At the age of sixty-nine, Jonna Frederiksen wasn't as strong as she used to be. Carrying her grocery bags to her bike alone was getting more and more difficult, but she did it. Jonna refused to let her age define her. She was still strong; she rode her bike downtown every day, where she went shopping or ran errands. She cooked for herself, and never had any outside help. She was in great health for her age, Dr. Williamsen told her every year at her yearly check-up. Her eyes weren't what they used to be, so she could no longer drive her car, but that didn't bother Jonna much. She loved riding her bike across Nordby and greeting her neighbors, as well as the tourists she met on her way. She loved the strong sea breeze and the smell of seaweed.

She walked out of the sliding doors of SuperBrugsen and put her grocery bag and purse in the basket on her bike. Then, she counted on her fingers. Six items. She knew she had to get six items today.

"Milk, coffee, a Swiss roll, lamb chops, green beans and potatoes." Yes she had everything she needed. Jonna never made a list before going to the store. That way, she was forced to remember what she needed. She just counted the items she needed to get, then forced herself to remember what they were. It was her way of keeping dementia as far away as possible. That was the only thing Jonna ever feared...losing her mind and not be able to remember her loved ones. Her mother had suffered from dementia for years before she died. Jonna was determined to never let it happen to her.

Jonna found the key and unlocked the chain on her bike. As she was about to pull the bike out onto the side-walk, a car suddenly drove past her, then stopped and backed up. A woman jumped out of the car and approached Jonna. She was tall and had broad shoulders. Jonna hadn't seen her before in the area and believed her to be a tourist. The woman had a map in her hand and started speaking in bad Danish.

"Please help me," she said. She put the map on the front of the car and asked Jonna to come closer and look at the map with her. "Please. Could you help? I need to find Mindevej."

Jonna scoffed. She looked skeptically at the woman. "There is no such thing as Mindevej here on the island," she said.

"Yes, yes," the woman kept saying. "Mindevej."

Jonna shook her head. She didn't move any closer to the woman, even though she kept asking her to come and look at the map.

I wasn't born yesterday, you know.

She glared at her purse in the basket, just as a man stepped out of the car as well. He spoke to her in a language she didn't understand. It sounded Eastern European. Jonna held on to her bike and started walking.

"I'm sorry. I don't understand what you're saying. I have to go..."

"Stop!" the man said.

There wasn't a soul on the street outside the store. No one to help if they tried anything. Maren, the cashier inside the store wouldn't be able to hear her if she screamed. A car drove by, but they didn't notice anything. Jonna didn't know them either. Probably tourists. Why people came to Fanoe Island at this time of year, she didn't understand. It was cold and clammy, and only someone who grew up here would fully be able to appreciate the cold wind biting the cheeks and the moist foggy air that came in from the North Sea. Still, she was always happy to see tourists. There hadn't been many this year.

"What do you want?" Jonna asked harshly. She had heard about these Eastern Europeans coming to Denmark since the borders were opened and robbing elderly people. She had heard the stories and read about them in the papers. But never had she heard about them coming to her wonderful small island.

The woman tried to talk and distract Jonna, while the man tried to put his hand inside her basket and grab her wallet. Jonna saw it and grabbed his arm holding the purse. She looked into his eyes while twisting his arm. Then, she grabbed his ear with the other hand and twisted it. She hadn't raised four grubby boys without learning a trick or two. The big man squirmed and crouched.

"Ouch!"

"So, you're trying to steal from an old woman, huh? Is that how your mother raised you? I bet she's very disappointed in you, young man. I know I would be. No son of mine would get away with attacking a skinny old woman on the street like this. How pathetic. Pick someone your own size next time. Now, let go of the purse, young man."

He did as he was told with a small whimper.

"Now I suggest you and that tramp of a woman you're holding on to, I suggest you get the hell out of here before I get really angry."

Jonna let go of the man and watched him sprint for the car. Seconds later, he and the woman and the gray station wagon were out of sight. Left on the sidewalk was Jonna with her purse in her hand and heart pounding heavily in her chest. She held on to her bike for a little while, catching her breath. Then she snorted and got on her bike. She started riding it down the street, shaking her head, and waving at her neighbors as she passed them.

"Attacking a poor old woman in broad daylight, is that what we've come to? Is that where this world is going? Someone ought to do something."

6

NOVEMBER 2014

"There was an old lady who was assaulted outside of SuperBrugsen today."

Morten and I were sitting in front of the TV watching a program about border patrol in Australia. Morten had come directly from work and told me he was staying the night. When I asked him how Jytte felt about that, he simply said *she'll live*. Morten had certainly changed in his approach to his daughter, and I was glad to feel she was no longer running the show. She was less fond of me than ever. To be frank, she hated my guts, but at least I had my boyfriend back. I had thought about asking him to move in, but knew we had to wait till Jytte moved away from home in a year or so. I still felt like he was spoiling her too much by giving her everything she pointed at, but had decided it was none of my business. Lord knows, my daughter wasn't the best behaved among girls either. They were just being teenagers. It was going to pass eventually, like everything else. Meanwhile, I was going to enjoy our life together, even if I couldn't take the relationship to the next level yet.

The officers on TV were searching a young backpacker

for drugs. Dogs were sniffing his belongings. They were my favorite part of the show.

"I always wanted a dog," I said.

"Were you even listening?" Morten asked.

I was leaning against his shoulder on the couch. "Yes, sorry. I heard you. A woman was assaulted?"

"A sixty-nine year old woman. She described the attackers as Eastern European. They tried to steal her purse. They've had a lot of trouble with these types on the mainland the last couple of years. I hope this doesn't mean they've found their way here. I really don't want this kind of stuff on our little island. It's bad for tourism and really bad news for us. Especially now that they're talking about cutting back on the police force."

"When will you know more about that?" I asked.

"Next week, I think. I tell you, I'm not looking forward to it."

"Is the woman alright?" I asked, as the dog found something and sniffed it closely. The officer pulled the dog back and started searching the pocket of the backpack. I loved the dogs. They always found something.

"Yes, apparently she chased them off."

"Who was it? Was she a tourist?"

"No, it was Jonna Frederiksen. She lives on the North side of Nordby. She was very shaken when I spoke to her, but not so badly she couldn't give me a very detailed description of the couple that assaulted her."

"I don't think I know her," I said.

"She's one of the real locals. You know, one of those that grew up here. Not moved here like you and me."

"I know. We'll never be real locals, not even if we live here for the rest of our lives," I said, laughing. There really was a distinction between those that had lived on the island for generations and those that had moved here. Even if it was your parent's generation that had moved here, you still weren't considered a local. That was just the way it was.

"Look at that dog. Look how smart he is," I said. "And adorable."

"He is very cute. I used to have a German shepherd once."

"For work?" I asked. "Was he a police dog?"

"Yes. I lost him to cancer. I loved that dog."

"Did you ever consider getting another one?" I asked.

Morten shook his head. "No. When you buy a dog, you also buy yourself some sorrow. They don't live long. It was rough on Jytte as well when he died. I don't want to put her through that again. You should get one, though. It would be good for Victor."

My eyes left the screen, and I looked at Morten. "Why, I think you might be on to something there, Detective. I've read about how being close to animals, especially dogs, can help kids with autism. I am looking to do something a little more radical. I've been looking into doing more about his diet. There are a lot of studies out there about how a gluten-free and casein-free diet can help his symptoms. Maybe this would be even better. I think I'll take him to the shelter tomorrow. Wow, I can't believe I hadn't thought about this before. He loves animals. Thanks."

Morten chuckled. "You're welcome." He leaned over and grabbed a cookie. The officer on TV was now pulling out bags of cocaine from the guy's bag, and he was starting to make excuses. I felt happy. In this moment, everything was just perfect. Well, maybe not perfect, but good. Real good.

7

MARCH 1959

BEING THE OLDEST, Ulrik Larsen was always a little concerned about awakening his father's wrath. It was easier for his two year younger brother Peter. Ulrik had, from a very early age, learned that he was responsible for both his and Peter's actions. That was just the way it was. So, if Peter got himself in trouble, Ulrik took the fall. It wasn't fair, but that's how life was, his father always said.

It seemed to Ulrik that life had been getting increasingly unfair ever since the baby had arrived. At thirteen, Ulrik was expected to be a grown-up. And act like one. So, when his father told him to go to old Hansen's house and ask if he need help, that's what Ulrik did. There was no room for complaining like Peter while they rode their bikes all the way across the dirt road and entered old Hansen's farm.

Old Mr. Hansen had fallen and broken his hip. That's all they had told Ulrik. And now, he couldn't work on his farm, so it was falling apart. He needed an extra pair of hands, Ulrik's father had said.

"Out here we take care of each other."

Ulrik loathed working with his hands. He knew it was his fate. He knew his father expected him to take over once he could no longer work. He was to run the farm. He had no choice.

Ulrik looked at his baby brother, who laughed and raced him to get there first. It was so unfair. Peter got to do whatever he wanted with his life. He could even go to college if he liked. Once he was done with high-school, Ulrik would come and work for his father. That was what was expected of him. It didn't matter that he hated working there. It didn't matter that the smell of pigs made him want to throw up, or that he loved to read books. Farmers didn't have time to read books. Farmers didn't go to college. Everything Ulrik was supposed to learn, his dad could teach him.

"I got here first!" Peter exclaimed, and made a skid mark in the gravel with his bike as he stopped. He threw Ulrik one of his bright and handsome smiles. It annoyed Ulrik how Peter had everything. Peter was going places. He would go see the world, visit museums, and read all the books he wanted, while surrounded by beautiful women all of his life. Meanwhile, Ulrik would be shoveling manure and smelling of pig. No wonder his dad was such a grumpy old man.

"Now, behave yourself," Ulrik said, as they parked their bikes, leaning them up against the wall of the white main building of the farm. A cold wind hit his face. Ulrik breathed in the breeze coming from the ocean not far away. He loved the sea breeze and dreamt of sailing away to exotic places.

Somewhere far far away from this island.

Ulrik didn't like Fanoe Island much. It was too desolate, he thought, and often dreamt of visiting big cities around the world. He dreamt of being surrounded by people, educated people who would discuss philosophy with him or art. He loved art. He wanted to visit museums and libraries all over the world. There was no culture out here in the countryside of the small island. Nothing but pigs and more pigs.

Ulrik was the first up the stairs, and his brother kept behind him as he knocked on the front door. "Let me do the talking."

Peter didn't argue. Neither of them were very happy to be at old Hansen's farm. The man had always scared them, especially when chasing them off his property shooting his rifle in the air when they were younger. They had spied on the old man and his wife, pretending to be secret spies shooting with peas in a sling at the wife, pretending to be shooting with guns. Those days were gone and old Hansen had only gotten older and angrier with age. Ulrik hadn't seen him in many years, not since his wife passed away. They had lost a child once, Ulrik's mother had told him. That's why they didn't like children on their property. The wife had never stopped crying about it. In the end, that's what killed her, Ulrik's mother had said. The sorrow killed her.

"What do you want?" The door was opened forcefully and a rifle was pointed at the two boys.

"Mr. Hansen? It's Ulrik. Ulrik and Peter Larsen. We're your neighbors?"

The old man chewed on tobacco and spat. "Ah, the troublemakers. What do you want?"

"Our dad sent us to ask if you needed any help around the farm. He heard about your accident." Ulrik looked down at the cane the old man was leaning against. He was holding the rifle clenched between his arm and chest. Only half of his face moved when he spoke. Ulrik's dad had told him that the man had a stroke. That's why he had fallen. It had numbed half of the man's face, and he looked crooked when he spoke. He seemed taken aback.

"Well...that's awfully nice of him, I guess. Well, you can start by feeding the dogs and the horse. I don't have many animals left, but those I have I can hardly take care of being like this. Then, if you could clean up in the barn over there. I can't get the car out and I can't bike downtown anymore with this hip. Your mother has been so nice as to bring me groceries whenever she went the last couple of days."

"Sure thing. Looks like we should take a look at the roof of your house as well," Ulrik said, when he spotted two buckets in the hallway behind the old man.

Mr. Hansen nodded with a deep sigh. "Yes. Yes, that would be nice of you. The storm in January took its toll on my old roof. Rains an awful lot at this time of year, huh?"

"I guess it does."

8

NOVEMBER 2014

LISA RASMUSSEN WAS PREPARING for war. Well, actually, it was just for the mayoral election that was coming up at the end of the month, but it felt just like she was going to war. Not just for her, but for her family as well.

She was making strategies, holding meetings, bribing the right people, and getting rid of those that weren't on her side. It was exhausting.

Lisa had her mind set on becoming Fanoe Island's next mayor, no matter the cost. This was her goal, this was what she had worked towards. And she had the public on her side. Every day, as she took her usual walk from her house in Nordby to city hall, she took her time to talk to anyone who wanted to. Even if it was just to exchange a few words, or to tell her how wonderful a job she had done cleaning up the town, or if it was to complain that the elderly weren't treated properly, that the food that was delivered by the city to their homes was bad. It didn't matter. Lisa took the time to listen to every problem and comment. She would grab their hands and shake them using both of hers, like she had seen presidents do on TV.

Now she was sitting in her house going through her strategies as her husband Christian entered the living room. He sat on the couch and put his feet up on the coffee table.

"Do you mind?" Lisa said. She looked at her papers. "I'm kind of in the middle of something."

"And I want to read the paper," he said with a grin. Ever since Lisa had gotten the idea that she wanted to be mayor, Christian had laughed at her. He didn't think she was ever going to be elected.

"The current mayor, Erling Bang, has been in his seat for many years. People love him. You don't stand a chance. People around here like things to stay the same. They don't like change."

Well, Lisa was just going to show him how wrong he was, wasn't she?

Christian sighed and took his feet down. "How long are we going to live like this?" he asked.

"What do you mean *live like this*?"

"You're never home. The house is a mess, look around. No one is at home to take care of the kids. I have to pick them up. You're never here, Lisa."

Lisa snorted. "Are you implying that I'm not a good mother?"

"No. You're a great mother. You just...well, you just haven't been around much lately. Amalie, Jacob, and Margrethe are all missing you. I miss you."

"You just miss me because I used to do all the work around the house, and now you have help out," she said.

"Well, yes. That too. It's hard on me to have to do everything. This morning, I ran out of clean underwear."

Lisa snorted again. "Didn't I just cook you dinner?"

Christian nodded. "Yes, yes you did."

"Didn't you enjoy it?"

"The meat was very tasty, yes."

"So, what are you complaining about? I've even hired a cleaning lady to clean up after you. I'll wash your clothes tonight. What is it again you do that is so hard?" Lisa stared at her husband with contempt. She really couldn't see the problem.

"Honey. We miss you, that's all. I know you take care of everything, but...well, even when you're home, this is all we get. You're always on the phone or writing or occupied with all this stuff. The kids are always asking for you. Every time we pass one of those posters on the streetlights when driving, they ask when this election will be over so they'll get their mother back. What do you want me to tell them? I mean, I don't think you'll win, but have you even thought it through? What if you win? You'll be so busy, we'll never see you. What about Margrethe? You're missing out on everything with her. Today, the teachers at the preschool told me she was crying because she missed her mother."

Lisa looked at her husband. "She was crying?"

"Yes. Apparently she hurt herself playing on the playground outside. The teacher didn't know how it happened, but she has a bruise on her back."

Lisa felt how her hand started to shake. "They don't know how it happened? Weren't they keeping an eye on her? Who did you talk to?"

"It was Laiyla. You know, the one with the piercing and purple hair."

Lisa broke the pencil in her hand. Yes, she knew her very well. Never trusted her much. Lisa closed her eyes and counted to ten backwards to calm herself down. Then, she looked at her husband again and smiled. Lisa tilted her head. She liked that they missed her. It was a good feeling. She put her hand in Christian's.

"I promise I'll try and be more present from now on, okay? So, Laiyla huh? And you say she wasn't paying attention to what our daughter was up to? Tell me everything she said."

9

NOVEMBER 2014

I took Victor and Maya to the shelter the very next day. They were both very excited in the car on our way there. Well, Maya tried hard not to be, but I could tell by the look on her face that she really was. Victor was smiling and looking out the window at the houses passing by. I was excited as well. This was an excellent idea. Just seeing their happy faces would make it all worth it, I was sure.

Nordby seemed desolate, I thought, as we parked close to the main street. It was always like this in the fall. All summer, the island was overrun by tourists; there was so much life, and when they departed, it was all calm and strangely empty. At least it seemed to be. There was plenty of activity still going on. The mayoral election was coming up, and all the streetlights were covered in posters for candidates. I still hadn't decided who I was voting for. They were down to two candidates. The sitting mayor, Mayor Erling Bang had been mayor for longer than anyone could remember. It was the first time in fifteen years that someone had gone up against him, I had been told. Lisa Rasmussen was his opponent. I liked the idea of change, and of having a woman in charge. I just wasn't quite sure about Lisa. She seemed a little fishy. I stared at her poster as we passed one. She seemed to be trying too hard to look gentle and trustworthy, but all I could see were those mad eyes of hers. They gave me the chills. I had no idea why.

It was dark, and grey clouds hung over our heads, but it hadn't started raining yet as we crossed the square. I was cold, even in my winter jacket. I nodded to a couple of people as we passed them. I knew most people by now. At least I recognized their faces. Like most Danes, the inhabitants of Fanoe Island didn't like to say hello, but they would nod with tight lips if your eyes accidently met. For the most part, people tried to not look at each other. Especially at this time of year when the cold made you bend forward slightly while walking, and all you really wanted was to sit inside by the fireplace or the TV with a cup of hot chocolate between your hands.

We passed a few small shops, the local real-estate agency, the small gas station, then continued down Niels Engersvej where I stopped in front of a small house. I looked at my phone where I had the address on the screen.

"This should be it," I said.

We walked up the small path leading to the front of the house. It was a couple that ran the place from their own home, I had read online. They took in sick animals, or animals that no one wanted and found new families for them.

A red-haired woman opened the door.

"Hi, I'm Emma Frost. I called about looking at a dog?"

The woman smiled. She seemed nice. She reached out her hand and grabbed mine. "I know who you are. Yes, come on inside. So, these two are the lucky children, huh?"

"Yes, well. We're just looking for now."

The red-haired woman laughed. "That's what they all say. But once you set your eyes on one, you can't let go. Come on in. I'm Camilla, by the way. My husband Poul is in the living room with the dogs. He brought them all into the playpen so you could take a look."

We walked inside, and the pungent odor of wet dogs and animal food hit my face. I could hear barking in the distance, and the sound of animals moving in cages.

"We have birds and cats as well, if there is any interest," Camilla said.

"I think we'll just look at the dogs for now," I said, and followed her into the living room. It was like a zoo in there. Birds jumping around in their cages, cats jumping around on the furniture, and dogs barking and biting each other inside the playpen. Victor and Maya rushed to the dogs and leaned on the fence. I spotted a small black dog that looked like it had some poodle in it. Poodles were smart dogs, I had read.

"That one is cute," I said and pointed. The small fluffy dog looked up and Camilla grabbed him and handed him to me.

"Oh, wow," I said, and held him close. He climbed up and licked my ear.

"He is very affectionate," Camilla said. "Loves children too. Fully potty-trained and up to date on his shots. He would be perfect. His name is Kenneth."

Maya came over and petted Kenneth on the head. "He's very cute," she said.

"And smart," Camilla said.

"I love that he is so small," Maya said.

"Small dogs are easy," Camilla said.

"I like him," Maya said.

"I like him too," I said, and petted him behind his ear. I

handed him to Maya, so she could try and hold him. He climbed up and licked her face. Maya laughed heartily. It had been awhile since I had seen her this happy. "Oh, my God, Mom, he really likes me."

"I'm sure he does." I let Maya hold Kenneth and looked at the other dogs in the pen. None of them were as cute as Kenneth. No, this was the perfect dog for us.

"So, I take it you have fallen in love?" Camilla said with a wide smile.

Maya looked up at me. "I love him, Mom. I really do."

"Well, I do too," I said, while looking for Victor. I spotted him standing in front of a big cage at the other end of the living room.

"Can we have him, Mom?" Maya continued.

I stared at Victor. He put his hand inside the cage.

"What is that down there?" I asked. "In the big cage."

Camilla looked concerned. "Oh, my. That's Brutus." Camilla walked towards Victor. "You shouldn't put your hand in there," she said, but Victor didn't listen. Camilla looked at me. "He really shouldn't put his hand in there."

I walked to him. "Take your hand out, buddy."

I looked inside the cage. A huge gray dog stared back with eyes as white as snow. It looked like a pit bull. It had scars on its face and only half an ear. I gasped. It looked really creepy.

"I'm sorry," Camilla said. "He's not safe. Please take your hand out of the cage before he bites you. He's been badly mistreated. He's not well. I'm afraid we might have to put him down soon. You can't trust him. He bit my husband just yesterday, attacked him out of the blue. He can't be trusted; no one will want him."

"I want him," Victor said.

Uh-oh. I had a feeling he would say that.

"No, you don't," Camilla said. "He's dangerous, sweetheart. Please, get your hand out." Camilla grabbed Victor's arm. I didn't realize until it was too late. Victor let out a loud scream. It was ear-piercing.

Camilla let go of his arm and looked at me.

"I'm sorry," I said. "He doesn't like to be touched."

The dog growled and banged his head against the bars while staring at Camilla. It looked like it was ready to kill her. Victor still had his hand inside the cage, but it didn't touch him.

"Now, he's doing it again," she said with terror in her voice. "Occasionally, he bangs his head against the bars like he's trying to get out. I really don't like that dog. It's very rare, since I love most animals, but this one I simply don't know how to handle."

"But he lets Victor pet him," I said.

"That's...that's the first time he ever let anyone touch him," Camilla said. "I've never seen him quite like this before. It's very unusual; normally, he never lets anyone touch him...just looking into his eyes usually makes him angry."

Exactly like Victor.

I turned to look at Maya, who was playing with Kenneth, throwing a small rubber bone across the room and having him fetch it for her. She was laughing and kissing the small dog. His ears flapped when he ran.

This is not good.

"I want this one," Victor said, still staring inside the cage and petting the dog. It was now licking his hand and calming down from his touch.

I sighed deeply. There was only one solution to this, and I was certain I was going to regret it.

"We'll take them both."

10

NOVEMBER 2014

The numerologist had just gotten back from her session with Maya. She threw her bag on the chair, then walked to the kitchen and grabbed a packet of crackers. She was tired. Tired of having to pretend like she liked that family and that awful person Emma Frost. Today, she had been close to just grabbing a kitchen knife and stabbing the terrible woman with it. Just finishing it then and there. The idiot had taken both of the children to the shelter and had come back with not one, but TWO dogs. The house was a mess and a zoo. The dogs were running all over the place, barking at each other, and fighting. Well, it was mostly the small black one that had been feisty, while the big grey one had been quieter, and simply sat in a corner staring at the numerologist and Maya like it was carefully planning how to attack them and eat them afterwards. The numerologist didn't known which was worse...the small dog constantly barking or the big quiet one staring at her with hungry eyes. Emma Frost had told her that she couldn't say no to either of them, and she had preferred the small black one, but Victor really had his eye on the big one, so she had taken them both.

The numerologist had felt like yelling at her, telling her how STUPID that was. How insane it was with two troubled children in the house. But she knew Emma Frost would never listen. She was simply too irresponsible.

The numerologist was happy to be home and put the laptop on her desk and opened it. Misty crawled across the table while the numerologist pulled out a cracker. Crumbs fell to the desk next to her laptop. Misty picked them up and ate them. The numerologist broke a cracker in two and handed one piece to the rat. It nibbled the cracker with great delight.

"There you go, sweetie."

The numerologist looked in her book and flipped a couple of pages. Things were going really well for her lately. Getting close to Emma Frost had been easy, and she had gathered a lot of material. Enough for her to take this to the next level. Yes, she had waited long enough. She wanted to move carefully, though. She wanted it all to happen in just the right way.

She flipped yet another page and drank from her water bottle. The stars were aligned just perfectly for her little plan to be fulfilled at this time. All predictions worked in her favor.

"See, Misty. All the books say the same thing," she mumbled, and stared into the computer screen.

It was true. 2014 was a special year. It was ruled by the number seven, since if you added all the numbers you got seven, making it a Universal Year.

The numerologist spoke while creating the web-page, sounding like she was trying to explain everything to her rat.

"The number seven is analytical and self-examining. It

starts a turnaround as, even the mind, as cold as it is, recognizes that duality doesn't benefit anyone."

She looked at the pyramid she had drawn on a piece of paper. A pyramid of numbers with the year and seven in the center. There was no doubt about what this pyramid was telling her. The five in the upper right side spoke very clearly. The five represented a big change or shocking and unexpected event around November of 2014, and if she looked it up, the stars would tell her it was caused in large part by miscommunication. The numerologist knew exactly what this miscommunication would be.

She ate another cracker and tapped on the keyboard. A picture of Emma Frost was found online, one where she was smirking during a book signing, then a small video from a TV show she was on once, talking about her books, where she laughed out loud. She edited it so it kept repeating her laughing, making her sound menacing. It was all placed on the page, and then accompanied by the text that the numerologist had carefully prepared.

"Yes, Misty. This is how it all starts. See, killing her for what she did is much too merciful, in my opinion. I want her to go down. I want her to hit the ground so hard she'll never get back up again. And then, we strike."

11

NOVEMBER 2014

OKAY, SO MAYBE I hadn't thought it through properly. Having one dog was a lot of work, but two dogs that were both new to the place was quite complicated, I soon realized. To my surprise, it wasn't the big one, Brutus, who caused me the most trouble. No, it was the small and gentle Kenneth that drove me nuts with all his barking and running around the house biting everything. He hadn't been in the house for more than ten minutes before he peed on the floor for the first time. In the living room. On the carpet. While I was cleaning it up, Maya came running and told me he had peed in the kitchen, and soon after, I stepped in a small puddle in the hallway as well. Frustrated and growling, I cleaned up again and again until I found one of my favorite shoes chewed into a thousand pieces in the bathroom.

"Maya!" I yelled.

She stuck her head inside the bathroom. "I think you should take him outside for a little bit. Take him out in the yard."

"But Victor is out there with Brutus right now," Maya said.

"They're dogs, for crying out loud. Can't they just play together?" I asked.

"I'm not sure the two of them should be playing together. Brutus could eat Kenneth in one bite without even chewing. And I think he wants to. That dog has been staring at Kenneth ever since we left that house like he really wants to taste him."

I exhaled. "Get a leash on him and take him for a walk down the street or on the beach. Just get him out of this house while I clean up after him."

"Okay," Maya said. She was about to leave, then stopped herself. "By the way, he pooped in the kitchen."

"Aaaargh! I thought he was supposed to be potty-trained!" I yelled, but Maya had left. I heard the front door slam, and suddenly the house was quiet for the first time since we got back from the shelter.

What have I done?

I finished cleaning up in the bathroom, then walked into the living room and looked at the damages. A pillow from the couch was shredded to pieces, Kenneth had left another puddle on the carpet, and tipped over my cup of coffee from this morning that I had left on the table.

I suddenly felt so incredibly tired. I sat down on the couch, thinking there was no way I was going to survive having these creatures in my house, when suddenly I heard a sound coming from the yard. I got up and walked to the window. Outside, between the trees, I spotted Victor and Brutus. What were they doing? Victor was sitting in front of Brutus, face to face, making it look like they were deep in conversation. I chuckled. Victor seemed so happy. I could hear him chatting with the dog. It was good for him to have something living to talk to for once. Usually, it was the trees and the rocks he spoke to, so this was, by far, an improvement, I had to admit. I didn't like the dog much still, especially not after Camilla had told me that they would take no responsibility if the dog were to hurt Victor or anyone else in the family. She really didn't recommend us taking the dog. She still wanted it to be put down.

Then, Victor stood up. He started walking around among the trees, and Brutus followed him. It looked like he was presenting Brutus to each and every tree in the yard. The strange part was how Brutus seemed to understand every word Victor spoke. Nah, that couldn't be. Maybe it just looked that way. Probably it was just an illusion, but the two of them definitely had created a bond...and very fast indeed. That was a good sign. I turned away and started cleaning the puddle and the coffee stains, and just as I had managed to put the living room back to normal, the front door opened and Maya yelled, "We're back!"

I took in a deep breath and braced myself for yet another couple of hours of complete chaos, as Kenneth's barking drowned out every thought in my mind. Seconds later, he whirled through the living room and started biting the edge of the couch, while growling at it like it had tried to attack him first.

12

NOVEMBER 2014

Annie Holmgren was in a hurry, as usual, as she drove the car off of the ferry onto Fanoe Island. She was a journalist at newspaper *JydskeVestkysten*, her office situated in Esbjerg with a view of The Wadden Sea with Fanoe peeking up in the horizon. She was happy to be one of those who had escaped the island. Growing up there was more than enough. She had known all of her life that she wanted to leave as soon as she was old enough. She wanted to have a career and make it big. So, she had...going to journalism school in Aarhus, the second biggest city in the country, then off to the biggest city, Copenhagen, for an internship at one of the big national newspapers and later hired as a reporter there. Having a career had been easy for Annie, easier than for her husband. She had met Bjorn at the newspaper where he worked as a photographer; they had worked on many stories together, and even traveled together. But soon after their wedding, and while their first child was on its way, Bjorn had been fired. Cutbacks, they said. He had started his own freelance company, but hadn't had many assignments. Once their first child, Maria, came along,

Bjorn had been a stay at home dad and Annie had cut her maternity leave in half so she could get back to her career. Bjorn had discovered that he liked it. He enjoyed being at home with their child. In fact, he had ended up taking care of all three children and the household while Annie focused on her career. Much to their surprise, they had both ended up liking their arrangement, him taking care of everything at home and her making the money. Yes, it was hard when they went to dinner parties and people asked him what he did for a living. It was tough on his ego. Especially in the eyes of his father-in-law. Annie's dad had never understood his choice. A man without a career, a man who didn't make money was hardly a man at all, he believed. And he never hesitated to tell Bjorn. It irritated Annie immensely, and over the years, she had visited her parents less and less. In the end, they only saw each other for Christmas.

When Annie's mother Elsebeth was diagnosed with cancer, everything had changed. Annie had realized her parents weren't going to be around forever, and she had quit her job at the newspaper and taken a job closer to the island at a smaller paper located in Esbjerg to be able to visit more often. She had helped out the best she could, since her father was old and not in the best health either. He was almost fifteen years older than her mother, and it was, therefore, the biggest surprise that she ended up dying before him. Annie had never had a close relationship with her father; she didn't know much about him except that he was born on Fanoe Island, had grown up on a farm outside of Nordby with his brother Peter, and had lived on the island all of his life. Ever since her mother died, she had tried hard to make up for the fact that she hardly knew him, but somehow, it felt like it was too late. Her father had been away most of her childhood, since he traveled a lot for his job. He had started his own company. Annie didn't know much about it except they sold machines to farmers all over Europe. She guessed it was tractors and such. Her dad never talked much with her or shared anything in detail. He had, however, been very disappointed in the fact that she was a girl, since he believed only a boy could take over the business. But when Annie's mother hadn't been able to provide another child after Annie, and when Annie had refused to take over the business that had kept her father away from her all of her childhood, her dad had, in bitterness, realized his company would die with him.

Annie hadn't wanted to go see him today; it hadn't been her plan, but she felt like she had to. She had plenty to do today and had to be in Vejle to do an interview in a few hours, but since they had called from the city and told her that her dad hadn't answered the door for days, and that it had been locked when the nurses tried to get inside, she felt she had to go and check on him. It wasn't that unusual. They had been through it before when her dad had refused to let the nurses in for up to a week at a time. It had happened several times before, Annie had said to the nice woman who had called, but still something inside of her felt stirred and uneasy. She knew she needed to quiet the anxiety she felt inside of her. So, she had pushed the interview back a little and hurried to catch the ferry.

Annie rushed through Nordby and drove up the hill onto the street of her childhood. She felt a chill as she parked the car in the driveway and got out. She looked across the street to number seventeen where Martin had lived. The handsome Martin that she had had a crush on for several years in school. She had heard he sold refrigerators now downtown. Annie shook her head. So glad she didn't end up marrying the guy. So happy she was one of those that got away. Staying here would have made her lose her mind. No doubt about it.

"Dad?" she yelled, as she knocked on the door.

There was no reply. The sign saying Ulrik Larsen on the door had fallen down on one side. A lot was falling apart on the house lately.

"Dad? It's Annie! Open up!"

Still, no answer. Annie sighed and found her own key to the house, then opened the door. Newspapers and letters coming through the mail slot had formed a pile behind the door and made it hard to push open.

This is a bad sign, Annie thought to herself. If anything, her dad always made sure to get the mail. He was a decent man who opened his mail and read the paper every single day.

Had he gotten hurt somehow? Has he fallen somewhere and can't get up? Oh my, is he in trouble?

"Daaad?"

No answer. She tried again. A revolting odor hit her. What the hell was that? What could smell like that? Had the freezer stopped working? Had there been a blackout and the meat had started to rot? Had he forgotten to change the cat's litter box? Where was the old cat anyway?

"Dad, where are you?"

Annie kept walking through the hallway towards the living room where her dad was usually sitting on the couch when she arrived. The same couch he usually refused to leave. The couch he would sleep on if the nurses let him. But this time, it was empty.

"Dad? Basse?"

That's odd. He never leaves the couch unless he has to.

A nervous feeling spread inside of her. No, there had to be some explanation. Ulrik Larsen was a very strong man.

He hadn't been sick in twenty years. Maybe he was simply still sleeping? It was, after all, still morning. But how would he have gotten into bed if the nurses hadn't been in to help him?

"Where are you, Dad? Are you in the bathroom?"

A fly landed on her forehead. Annie wiped it away. Another one buzzed her face. Soon three, then four.

Flies? At this time of year?

She had walked back into the hallway towards the bedroom when she heard a strange sound coming from the kitchen. A buzzing sound.

The sound of a thousand flies. Oh, my God!

Part of her was screaming to get out of there as soon as possible, but she felt like she was frozen. Like she was paralyzed. She was drawn towards it. She had to know. As she peeked inside the kitchen, holding her scarf up against her nose and mouth, her eyes started watering. Not because of the horrendous odor, but because of what she saw. Her own dad lying on the tile floor in a pool of blood. Flies were buzzing around him and his old cat, Basse, was gnawing on his face.

13

MARCH 1959

ULRIK AND PETER worked at old Hansen's farm all weekend, and the following Saturday their dad asked them to go down there again. Ulrik and Peter did as they were told without asking any questions. Old Hansen was happy to see them and immediately asked them to feed the horse and the dogs and clean up outside the main building.

"I'll take the horse, you feed the dogs," Ulrik said to his younger brother.

It was a nice spring day with clear skies and crisp air. Ulrik enjoyed being outside. He took the horse out in the paddock. The horse jumped and ran off while Ulrik closed the fence. Then he cleaned out the horse's stall and gave it fresh straw and hay. He poured food in the trough, and then returned to see if his brother needed help with the dogs. Peter was playing with the big labs in the farmyard. He had found a ball that he was throwing and the three labs ran to get it. Peter was laughing when they ran back to him and jumped on him. Then he grabbed the ball out of the mouth of one dog and threw it again. The three dogs all ran for it. Peter laughed. Ulrik smiled at the sight of his brother enjoying himself. There weren't many times either of them got to play or be childish anymore. Ulrik had watched his brother for a little while, when he realized he wasn't the only one watching him. On the stairs outside the house stood Mr. Hansen. He was leaning on his cane while staring at Peter. He was smiling too. There was something about the way he looked at Peter that made Ulrik feel uncomfortable.

Ulrik walked into the courtyard and yelled at his brother. "Enough fooling around. Come help me carry these big tires over here into the barn."

Peter left the dogs and ran to help his brother. They carried the tires inside the barn, and then walked back to clean up the pile of old garbage. All the while, Ulrik couldn't escape the feeling that old Hansen was observing them, monitoring their every move.

"What happened to Hansen's child?" Ulrik asked at the dinner table when they returned that night.

His parents exchanged a look. His dad dropped his fork onto the plate. "That's none of our business, son," he answered.

"He died when he was twelve, I heard," Ulrik continued, even though he knew it was a touchy subject.

His mother tightened her lips and shook her head. "We don't talk about it. Eat your potatoes."

"Why?" Ulrik said. "Why can't we talk about it?"

"It was a tragedy," his mother replied. "We don't talk about people's tragedies. It's also a bad omen to talk about the dead."

"What kind of tragedy?" Ulrik continued.

He could tell by the look on his father's face that he was pushing it now. His mother saw it as well. She looked at her husband before she answered.

"An accident. The boy fell or something; now, eat your potatoes."

"Fell how?" Peter had become curious as well now.

Their mother sighed, annoyed. "I don't know. We don't talk about it. It's none of our business."

"I heard he was trampled to death by the cows," Ulrik said. "That's why they got rid of all the cows afterwards."

"I heard he fell from the roof," Peter said. "That he was trying to run from the ghost that haunts that place. A ghost that kills children. It's true. He lives here on the island. He watches them for a long time, and then he lures them into the forest before he kills them. At least that's what some kids are saying."

Their mother looked perplexed, then cleared her throat. "Well, that's all very nice, but as far as we know, it was just an accident and it was very rough on the family. Let's not talk any more about this. Some things are best left in the past. Now, eat your dinner. You're going down there again tomorrow, your father said. I think you're doing a great thing helping the old man out. Now, eat."

14

NOVEMBER 2014

THAT NIGHT I HAD A NIGHTMARE. I dreamt of this strange figure hiding between the trees in my yard watching Victor. He was tall and had no face. He was wearing a suit and tie. His long slender arms were stretching out to grab Victor just as I woke up with a loud scream. I gasped for air, then screamed again. Right next to my bed sat Brutus in the light from the full moon outside my window. His white eyes were staring directly at me. My heart was pounding heavily as I crouched on the corner of my bed. I turned to look at the door. It was closed.

"How did you get in here?" I said.

The dog kept staring at me. He looked like he wanted to kill me. Those white eyes were creepy.

"What do you want?"

The dog didn't make a sound. That was almost the scariest part about him...that he was so quiet. It was like he was observing us, maybe planning his move on how to kill us all.

"Get out!" I said.

The dog didn't move. I pointed at the door. "Get out of here."

I got up and grabbed his collar. Brutus growled loudly and snapped at me. I gasped and let go, then jumped onto the bed.

"Victor!"

Victor came into my room, rubbing his eyes. "Brutus!" he said, and hugged the dog. The pit bull didn't make a sound.

"Would you get him out of here?" I said.

Victor looked the dog in the eyes. For a few seconds, they stood like that, and I could have sworn they were communicating somehow. It freaked me out.

"Just get the dog out of here, now!" I said.

Victor turned around and walked out of the door without a sound. The dog immediately followed. I threw myself on the bed as I exhaled, and then went back to sleep, thinking that dog was going to be the end of us all.

"I swear to God, the dog wants to kill me," I told Sophia when she came over for coffee later. The kids were off to school, and I was alone with the two beasts. I couldn't decide which one of them was worse. Kenneth was eating one of Maya's shoes, while Brutus was sitting in the corner staring at us, looking exactly like one of those porcelain dogs. It gave me the chills. I turned away and looked at Sophia instead. She laughed.

"It seems like you're in a little over your head here," she said.

"I told the kids that they need to take care of them on their own. I'll walk them once during the day, and let them into the yard before nighttime, but they have to walk them in the morning and in the afternoon. Those were the terms.

I'm not taking care of that pit bull over there. He'll eat me in one bite."

"You know that's not going to last," Sophia said with a grin. "In a few days, you'll be stuck with walking and feeding and bathing the both of them."

I sipped my coffee and grabbed a bun that I had managed to bake this morning, even though the house had been in chaos, with Kenneth peeing on the floor and eating the furniture and Maya running after him screaming and yelling that she was in a hurry and that she needed to fix her hair. It was quite the circus.

"I'm taking them back, then," I said. "I can't take care of two dogs. There's no way. Especially not that quiet one over there. He freaks me out, I tell you."

I buttered my bun. Sophia grabbed one as well. Nothing like a second breakfast with your best friend. Sophia looked really well. I guessed it was the love between her and Jack. She had just been so happy lately. I was really thrilled for them. Really. Even though I had to admit that I might have been slightly, only slightly, jealous. I hadn't had that spark in my relationship with Morten for a long time. We were doing well, yes. Better than a few months ago, but still, I felt like something was missing. I couldn't put my finger on it. Maybe I was just bored. We needed to spice things up a little. I had thought about it for a long time and planned something special. Tonight, I was taking him to folk dancing class downtown. Yes, we were going to learn the local Fanoe-dance, and he had no idea.

My phone rang. It was Morten. He sounded agitated. "I'm sorry, sweetie. I won't be able to make it tonight."

"Aw!"

"I know. But something's come up. They found a body."

My eyes widened. "Who? What?"

"I'll tell you details later. I'm on my way down there."

END OF EXCERPT

ORDER YOUR COPY TODAY!

Made in the USA
Monee, IL
20 September 2021

78432435R00173